JENNER

The K9 Files, Book 16

Dale Mayer

JENNER: THE K9 FILES, BOOK 16
Beverly Dale Mayer
Valley Publishing Ltd.

ISBN-13: 978-1-773365-51-0
Print Edition

Books in This Series

About This Book

Welcome to the all new K9 Files series reconnecting readers with the unforgettable men from SEALs of Steel in a new series of action packed, page turning romantic suspense that fans have come to expect from USA TODAY Bestselling author Dale Mayer. Pssst… you'll meet other favorite characters from SEALs of Honor and Heroes for Hire too!

Heading to Ashland, Kentucky, where his ex-wife's family lives, is not in Jenner's plans anytime soon. But, given a War Dog is potentially in trouble, well, Jenner will even face his past. Arriving at a small bed-and-breakfast, he meets a woman more interesting than anyone he'd met in a long time. His job to find this missing dog seems like a long shot, until he learns about the B&B neighbor's son and his pack of dogs, who have been scaring Kellie …

Kellie loves her bed-and-breakfast establishment, as much as she loves meeting new people, particularly when she doesn't have a great relationship with many of the locals, who judged her harshly for a past mistake. Determined to enjoy life regardless, she tries to move on but finds it hard to leave her past behind. And now there's her neighbor …

Having Jenner around makes Kellie feel more secure and gives her hope that maybe good people still exist in this world. Yet, before they can truly move forward, there is a canine issue, … and a neighbor with something else on his mind …

Sign up to be notified of all Dale's releases here!
https://geni.us/DaleNews

PROLOGUE

B ADGER READ THE text and looked over at Kat. "Wow, look at that," he said, holding up his phone, showing the text message of the heart emoji.

"Ah, looks to me like we have another happy success story. It just blows me away that it's happening time and time again." She smiled, looking over at him.

"I know. So who do we have next?"

"You want me to look?" she asked.

"Yeah. Do you know anybody who needs rescuing?"

"I don't know about rescuing, but I have a case that's driving me crazy."

"What do you mean by a case?"

"Somebody who isn't adapting well to his prosthetics because he's pushing them too hard," she admitted.

"What's he doing?"

"Tons of outdoor hiking, survival-type stuff," she noted. "He's all over the board. He brought me back one of the latest titanium prosthetics that was damn near broken." Badger stared at her in shock. "Well, he's also big," she added, "and I guess I hadn't made quite enough allowances for that."

"How big?"

"Six feet two," she replied, "and I suspect, with both legs, he would be somewhere around two-sixty."

"Right." Badger nodded. "That's big. Does he like dogs?"

"I can ask him."

"Sure, ask away. What does he do for a living?"

"He's ex-navy," she stated. "Why?"

"Because I don't have anybody around here to recruit. We've pretty well tapped out all our resources, at least for the moment, though we always have new guys coming and going. But you know what? We do have another missing War Dog."

"I could ask anyway. He seems to keep himself so busy because he has nothing else to do."

"Does he know anything about dogs but also horses, cattle, or anything like that?"

"Why?"

"Because it sounds like this War Dog was taken to a ranch in Kentucky," he explained.

"What happened to it?" she asked, astonished.

"Nobody knows. It just disappeared."

"Coyotes?"

"Not likely," he said.

"Is this dog injured?"

"No, it seemed to be healthy, but, according to everybody we've talked to, it just vanished."

"You don't sound like you believe that."

"Nope, I sure don't. Not if the dog was well treated."

"And, of course, that's the trick, isn't it?" she stated. "Not only do you have to find sincerely good people but you also have to find someone the dog bonds with."

"I'm thinking that, in this case, we have a problem because the wife died, and the dog was basically bonded to her."

"Of course, and now the dog is dealing with yet another loss."

"Exactly," Badger agreed. "I need somebody who'll give the dog an outdoor life."

"Well, maybe my client would be a good fit," she suggested. "I can ask him."

"What's his name?"

"Jake," she said. "No wait." She stopped and reconsidered that. "Jenner. It's Jenner."

"Not a problem," Badger said. "Give him a call."

She grabbed her phone and called him. He sounded surprised to hear from her. "Have a question or two," she stated. "I know you're really active outdoors, but I just wondered if you ever had any experience with dogs."

"Of course," he said. "Why?"

"My husband has been dealing with some of these retired K9 War Dogs. I think I told you about that."

"Yeah, I heard something about it. So, what's up?"

"A dog in Kentucky went missing, and we were sitting here brainstorming, trying to find somebody willing to make a trip up there to take a look for the dog."

"Why Kentucky?" he asked, his voice hard.

"The dog may be at a ranch there." She hesitated and asked, "Is that triggering something for you?"

"Yeah, … my ex-wife is there."

"Ah," Kat replied, "so I gather you're not the right person for this job."

"I don't know," he stated. "What's involved?"

"Well, no money for one thing," she noted. "I can tell you that."

"I don't need money," he said quietly.

"I know. It's one of the reasons why I thought about

you. We just need somebody to go see what happened to the dog. I mean, if it died or something, that's one thing. Or if it's been adopted by somebody else and is happy, that's all good. But if it's suffering out there somewhere, we need it brought into a better situation. You mentioned your ex-wife. What kind of scenario did you leave behind?"

"She didn't like military life and chose somebody else instead," he noted quietly.

"Ouch, I'm sorry."

"Yeah, me too," he said. "I haven't spoken to her since."

"Maybe it's time to make peace?"

He hesitated. "Maybe, … not exactly what I was thinking I would be doing."

"No, but how do you feel about a dog in need?"

"That," he replied, "I would do in a heartbeat."

"That makes you the right man for the job then," she stated. "I'll pass you over to Badger now. And by the way," she said, before she handed the phone over, "what is your wife's name?"

"Laura," he said. "Why?"

"*Huh*, that's a nice name."

"She's a nice woman, or at least she was."

"Are you sure she remarried?"

"I don't know," he replied, "but she divorced me pretty damn fast."

"Maybe she just needed to know that you would come home one day."

"Well, I did, and she wasn't expecting it. Or maybe she was afraid I'd come home in pieces, like I did," he admitted, his voice even harder.

"Pieces that you've been working really hard at putting back together," she added.

"Yeah, but, as you know, nothing is perfect about any of it."

"Nothing is perfect in life at all," she reminded him. "It's all about progress."

"Well, if I can help a dog, I'm happy to," he said. "Besides, it'll stop me from going crazy. I'm kind of growing tired of all the hikes."

"That doesn't sound normal for you."

"No, I know," he admitted. "I guess maybe I'm just missing something in life."

"Yeah," she agreed, her voice soft as she whispered, "You're missing Laura."

"Doesn't matter if I'm missing her or not," he snapped. "She made a choice, and it didn't include me."

"Maybe you need to go see *why* she made that choice," she added, her intuition kicking in.

"Maybe," he admitted. "If nothing else, it'll be good to call it quits, to look at my past, and to move forward again," he noted. "For that reason alone, I should probably do this. I'll do it because I need to," he added, "but I'll enjoy it because I get to help an animal. That makes it worthwhile to me."

And with that, she said, "Good enough, now here is Badger."

CHAPTER 1

J ENNER MORRISON DROVE down through the horse ranches, long green pastures, and white fences, shaking his head. "Is there any other place quite like Kentucky for horses?" he murmured out loud.

The area was still postcard picturesque. Just as he remembered Ashland.

But then, hey, he hadn't been here in many, many years. Not since his ex-wife had divorced him, and, at first, he'd thought she had married his best friend. He'd heard soon afterward that it was somebody different. Still, his supposed buddy had confessed to sleeping with Laura, just not marrying her, and so Jenner had also ditched his best friend at the same time.

At the airport, Jenner had picked up the rental truck, wanting space for a large dog crate, if needed. His main concern was finding the War Dog named Sisco. A male that had had several broken ankles apparently, according to his file, all healed, yet he'd lost his speed. Although he still had the perfect training at that point in time, he'd been adopted out. Which was good for him because he got to live the rest of his life in retirement. But what happened to him after that was a whole different story. And this all happened to Sisco a town over from where his ex-wife now lived.

As Jenner drove along more huge green pastures and

white fences, he just smiled. Something was so very familiar about all this. He'd been raised on a horse farm, had many happy years here, until the family had sold it after his mother's death. She'd been the horse-crazy one, and his father had always hated the farm part. She had died from a head injury, caused by a fall while out riding. Still, Jenner certainly didn't blame the horse.

As it was, they'd moved to the opposite side of the country, California, and that's where he'd signed up for the navy and had met Laura soon afterward. Only she'd been from this area, and, as they'd spent a lot of time back-and-forth with her family and with his, this still always remained one of Jenner's favorite locations. It kind of blew him away that he was even back here again. After what? Seven years? Nine?

He drove up to the bed-and-breakfast that he'd booked for this odd trip down memory lane. "Focus on the dog, not the memories," he muttered to himself. He pulled up in front and parked.

Horse Happy was the name of the place. He shook his head.

"*Horse Nuts* would be a better name. After all, that's what everyone around here is," he muttered. He hopped out of the truck, grabbed his duffel bag, and walked in the front entrance. It was a long two-story structure with four dormers and a big wraparound veranda. The yellow-and-white trim added to the bright yet cozy *come stay with us* vibe. He liked it. Big double doors opened to a huge reception area, with a small desk beside the stairs, that was aimed upward.

A woman looked up and smiled at him. "Hey, I'm Kellie Spalding. Welcome to my home." She asked him, "Do you have a reservation?" He nodded and gave her his name. "Okay, I do have you down here." She frowned, as she looked at the booking, and he waited for the inevitable questions. "I don't have down the number of nights that you're staying." She looked up at him. "Will this be just an overnight stay?"

He shrugged. "No, it'll be at least two. Possibly a week. If you have room."

"That's fine. I'll give you the front room, on the second floor." She handed him a key, pointed at the stairs, and added, "Dinner is included, as is the continental breakfast. Unless you have other plans, I'll see you for dinner at five o'clock." She glanced at her watch and frowned. "Which means I need to get to the kitchen pretty soon," she said, with a bright laugh.

She held out the credit card machine. He paid for the first night. "I'm pretty easy to feed." Careful of his limp, he moved slowly toward the stairs and up. His leg was especially sore after the drive. He felt her curious gaze following him, but, when he got to the room in question, he used the key and stepped inside. A large double bed, a big double window, and a window seat. Plus a lovely rug at the foot of the bed. That was all good.

He dropped his duffel bag on the bed, walked over to the big double window, and sent Badger a text message. **I'm here.** And, with that, he pulled out his laptop, looked around, and noted a small recliner chair but no side table.

With another assessing look, he emptied one of night tables and moved it over, so he could put the laptop on it while he sat. Hardly the best scenario, but it would work in the short term. Then he sat down and brought up a map of Sisco's past locations.

The area wasn't very far from here, within walking distance. With that knowledge, he grabbed his phone and headed back downstairs. When he got to the bottom, he felt his prosthetic ankle kicking slightly offside. He swore at that.

Kellie, still at the front desk, looked at him anxiously. "Problems?"

He faced her, frowning. "Unless you have an Allen wrench, it could be."

Her eyebrows shot up. "Absolutely no problem. I do have one?"

"Yeah, if you've got one," he replied. She disappeared into another room, and he followed her slowly. When he saw a half-open door to a den, with a couple tables and easy chairs, he asked, "Is this room for the guests?"

"Yes, absolutely," she said, "plus the large dining room down here, and then we have the kitchen around the corner. Do you need a space?"

"I'm looking for a place to work on my laptop."

"Oh, easily done. Pick a spot. Anywhere you're comfortable."

"Not an issue now, but good to know. I planned to go for a walk around the area right now, until dinner is ready. That's when you heard me cursing my ankle."

She stopped and stared at him and slowly handed him the Allen wrench. He looked down at it, walked over to a chair, and sat. He lifted his ankle across his other knee and pulled up his pant leg.

"Oh my," she said immediately.

He was so accustomed to this prosthetic. It was an older model that he'd decided to travel with, while Kat worked on adaptations to his newer ones. "Yeah, sometimes the mechanics don't work so well. It is an older model."

He quickly shifted where the metal had been grating on the moving parts and, using the Allen wrench, adjusted the joints. He hopped to his feet and moved around a bit, bending and extending his leg. He walked back to the stairs, walked up a few, turned around, and walked back down again. And then he returned the wrench to her. "Thanks."

She took it willingly and added, "That looks like quite an injury you must have had."

"Just one of multiple at the same time," he replied agreeably. "I was in the navy. We were doing war games on a small Zodiac, when we took on a little more than we expected in terms of damage," he explained. "But I'm here, and I'm alive and well. That's all that matters,"

"I'm glad to hear that," she noted, concern on her face.

"Are there any local general stores or something nearby that's walkable?"

She shook her head at that. "No, we're far out from the closest town for walking purposes. Not sure what you're looking for in particular, and I don't know how far you're planning on going. Do you need me to push back dinner for you?"

"No, of course not. It's not that big a deal," he stated. "I was just wondering about a property close by here."

Her eyebrows rose slowly. "Are you looking at buying?"

"No, I'm looking for a War Dog last seen in the area." At that, her face creased, in a way that amazed him. She would never be any good at poker because her every expression showed. So far, he'd seen shock, curiosity, relief, and now more curiosity.

"War Dog?" she asked cautiously.

"Yeah, a dog adopted by one of the locals," he noted. "It was a special dog from one of the overseas K9 units."

"Oh." She still frowned, now shook her head at that. "I'm not even sure which neighbor would have done that," she murmured. When he gave her the name Stippletone, she added, "Well, they're here, just a little bit down the road, but I don't remember them having any kind of fancy dog."

"I don't think it would look like a fancy dog at all," he replied. "At least not at this point in time. He looks like a normal dark-coated shepherd."

She nodded slowly. "I guess that makes sense. The Stippletones always seemed to have a number of dogs around."

"So you don't know anything about this one, I guess?"

"No, I don't." She frowned. "I'm not sure that's the family you want though."

"Why's that?" he asked, stopping as he reached the front door.

"The main family or the original family were really good people," she stated, then hesitated. "I guess that's really not something I should be talking about."

"Please," he urged her. "I'm here on a welfare check to make sure the animal is okay."

Her lips formed a tiny rose bud. And then she shrugged. "I guess you'll probably hear it from the locals anyway, but the older couple was killed in a car accident."

He stared at her. "Both of them? Seriously?"

She nodded.

"Was that maybe two months ago?"

"About that, yeah," she agreed, "and they were really good people. They'll bend over backward to help anybody. Couple of times I've run into a bit of trouble, and they immediately helped. Now, they have a son, but I don't know much about him."

"Is there anybody else left in the family?"

She shook her head. "I don't know of any other siblings."

"So he may have the dog himself."

"He might," she replied, with a nod. "The family did like dogs—not unruly ones—but there are quite a few dogs there now with the son. I don't ..." She hesitated and crossed her arms on her chest.

He watched her body language with interest. "Obviously something about this bothers you."

"It's the dogs that bother me," she admitted. "Believe you me. I'm an animal lover but a lot of these? I just get the feeling that ... well, let me just say, I went for a walk one evening, and I got surrounded by them, and I was definitely scared. They were out of control, and I don't know what they would have done if the son hadn't been there to call them back."

At that, Jenner frowned. "That doesn't sound good."

"No, and when I saw him later, he told me that I had just let my fears get ahold of me."

"But you should never be afraid of dogs like that. When surrounded, however, it's hard not to be. A pup can be dangerous. Now the War Dog is not the same. It's been well trained. If he's been well treated, he wouldn't attack in a situation like that, particularly a War Dog that has extensive military training."

"Well, the old owners, the couple? They raised shepherds for decades," she shared. "I know that they were really very, very capable. I'm just not so sure about the son."

"They wouldn't have had the War Dog for very long," he noted. "I think it was only adopted about six months ago. And then, when the welfare check came through, nobody knew anything about its whereabouts."

"I don't know about that either," she stated. "The son seems to buy and sell animals, so he may very well have sold the War Dog."

"That's not allowed in the contract."

"But the contract would likely had been with his parents, who are now deceased," she pointed out.

Jenner nodded thoughtfully. "That could be why the welfare check didn't go through and why the dog was flagged for a house call."

"I'm really glad to hear that the government is checking up on these animals," she stated warmly, "because they've done so much for our country. So you really want to confirm that they're being well looked after."

He nodded. "And I never was somebody who could leave an animal in need." He looked over at her again, considering what she had said and what she wasn't saying. "Did you have any trouble with the son?"

Again her arms clenched, as they wrapped around her chest. Then she shrugged. "I don't want to cause any trouble."

"You're not causing any trouble," he stated firmly. "Perhaps you should just tell me what it is that makes you uneasy, besides the dogs, obviously."

She nodded. "The dogs are definitely a part of it, but I guess, when it comes to him, there's just something I don't like."

"In what way?" She just shook her head. "Please," he urged her, "I need to know what I'm dealing with."

"I don't like the way he looks at me."

At that, he took a step back. "Do you feel like you're in danger?"

"I don't feel safe. There's just something ..." She stopped, tilted her head, and added, "I don't know, *smeary*."

"*Smeary*?" he asked. "Not sure I know that word."

"Just ... *slimy* may be a better word. I don't know. Something makes me want to take several steps back from him anytime I'm alone with him. He really crowds me too."

"Meaning, he likes to step into your personal space?" Jenner asked, as he took several steps toward her.

She immediately backed up, nodding. "Yes, that and he comes here, even though I'm closed. He rang the doorbell a couple times, when he's been really drunk. And it made me feel really uncomfortable."

"And so you would be." He looked around. "Do you have much for security?"

She shook her head. "Not a whole system. I do have a camera on the front door. I mean, we never have any problems in this area," she explained. "It's just been recently."

"Do you have other guests staying here?"

"No, not right now," she confirmed. "I do have two couples coming in on the weekend."

"Okay." Jenner nodded. "So it's just you and me for the next few days."

She nodded, as if uncertain about the way he had said that.

KELLIE SPALDING LOOKED at her new guest, even as he studied her. She had been more than surprised to see his prosthetic leg because she had seen no indication, except for a slight limp. And now just the talk about a War Dog reminded her what she'd gone through last time, the gripping fear, as she had been surrounded by those dogs. She rubbed her arms. "Look. I don't want to cause any trouble, but he's the kind of guy I choose to avoid, if I can."

"Got it." As he opened the front door, he asked, "Any idea how many dogs he has?"

"Last I saw, three, four, maybe five even," she replied.

"And that's how many surrounded you?"

She nodded. "Yes, well, four seemed to be more aggressive, while one kinda hung back," she said, with a headshake. "I don't remember any of them being a shepherd."

"What about his parents' dogs?"

"They were down to just the one at the end. I remember her saying something about a charity dog."

"That could have been Sisco, the military dog," he noted thoughtfully.

"And they were the kind of people who would have definitely taken it in and would have even applied for that honor. He was military himself, and I know he always wanted to be of service in some way or another."

"That makes sense then," Jenner noted. "We don't always know what happens when a War Dog is adopted. However, legally it would have been adopted by the parents, not necessarily the son."

"Right," she murmured. "The son isn't the most agreeable person."

"I don't really care how agreeable he is, as long as the War Dog's in good shape and is happy there."

She nodded. "Well, I'll let you get walking. You plan on being back in time for dinner?"

"I'll be back in time," he said. "I'll just go down to your neighbors' place and see what I can see."

CHAPTER 2

KELLIE WATCHED AS Jenner headed out the door. The limp was less pronounced now, or so she hoped. It would mean she'd helped in a small way. He was no longer in her sight, but she remained on the porch, just taking in the scenery. She loved it here. As she watched, another vehicle drove up. She smiled when the car door opened, and a fully pregnant Laura wiggled out. "Hey," she greeted her friend, as she walked down her front steps, closer to Laura. "How's life?"

"It's fine," Laura snapped, with an irritable shrug. "Just too much going on these days."

"I'm sorry to hear that," Kellie replied. Laura often had a less-than-positive outlook on life. Even though she had so much going for her.

"I am too." Laura let out a slow breath.

"You want to come inside and sit down?"

Laura shook her head. "Hey, sorry. I'm not trying to be a bitch, just had a really crappy day."

"I'm sorry for that too," Kellie noted. "You aren't usually this irritated."

"No, I'm not," she agreed. "Got this phone message from my ex-husband, wanting to meet. I was trying to avoid that for a very long time, but apparently I don't get to avoid it anymore." She shook her head. "Although, if I'm lucky, maybe he'll leave town without contacting me."

"Is it a problem?"

"I don't know whether it's a problem or not," she said. "Leaving him was definitely what I needed to do back then. I didn't give him much of an explanation for leaving him, not sure I even have much of an explanation for it right now either—except I was young and stupid."

"Bring Silas in on it. Or does he not know?"

Now Laura was pacing the driveway, with one hand at her lower back. "That I don't want to do. He doesn't like the fact that I was married before, in the first place."

At that, Kellie nodded. She'd heard some of this before, not a whole lot of it though. She and Laura had been friends of a sort for at least five years now. And Laura's marriage to Silas was something that doesn't come up. Deliberately. They were an odd couple at the best of times. "Sorry for anything that brings you stress," Kellie said. "It's something you don't need, especially now." She pointed to her friend's large belly.

"Nope, I sure don't," she agreed, as she patted her baby bump. "I don't have a clue what brought my ex into town or why he's even contacting me, but it's not what I expected. And, of course, anything unexpected makes me nervous."

"Of course," Kellie agreed gently, "but, if there were no hard feelings about the breakup, I'm sure that's not an issue."

"I didn't say there weren't any hard feelings. I was not the person I am now," she added, and with that came such an odd tone in her voice.

Kellie looked at her friend and frowned. "Ouch. I gather you aren't terribly happy about some issues?"

She shook her head. "No, sure not." Laura huffed. "Trouble is, I'm not even sure how to explain who I was back then, and I never expected to have to explain it to him."

"Who says you need to?" Kellie asked. "Just tell him that you don't want to meet. Tell him it's old water under the bridge, and you've moved on."

"He knows I've moved on," she noted. "I just don't know that he understands why I walked away. And, of course, what I told him back then wasn't the truth, and I know it's brought some hardship with his own friend because I had told him that I was marrying him. His best friend no less."

"Wow." She stared in fascination at Laura. Normally the woman was a very well-put-together person, but today she appeared to be quite rattled. "Sounds like maybe there is a reason to meet him then, if for no other reason so that you don't have to avoid him for the rest of your life."

"He's in the navy, been working out of California for a lot of years," she replied in exasperation. "So I never expected to see him again." Then, with an irritated shrug, she added, "Of course he shows up now."

Not sure what to say about that, Kellie just nodded. "So why are you here today?"

"I'm wondering if you have reservations for the week when the baby's due?" she asked. "My family wants to come, but, of course, Silas doesn't want them at the house."

"Ah," she said, as she brought up her booking schedule on her phone. "And your due date's what? Six weeks from now?"

"It is," she said, frowning at her tummy. "The problem is, I don't know that Junior here will respect his due date in any way, shape, or form. So the booking must be fluid."

Kellie thought about it and added, "I do have some flexibility because that's an October deadline. It's just the beginning of September now, and it generally calms down by then."

"Well, it's pretty empty right now, isn't it?"

"It has been," she agreed, "but I had someone new in today, and I have two couples coming in this weekend."

"Good enough," Laura said. "It will be for two couples because my brother and his wife will come, and my parents wanted to come too."

"I'll put down a tentative booking for you for two rooms."

"Make it more than *tentative*. I won't be too happy—if you end up full, and there's no room for them right around when they arrive—and I have to deal with Silas."

"What if the due date changes?"

"The only thing I can tell you is what I have for a due date now," she snapped. And, with that, she turned and headed back to her car. She was massaging her lower back, as she took a couple more steps.

"How is the pregnancy going?" Kellie asked.

"It's going fine," she replied, "which, you know, considering I'm in my early thirties, it's about time I got started."

At that, Kellie winced. She was in her early thirties herself. She didn't have a partner and hadn't contemplated a family because … it made things a little more complicated.

She watched as Laura drove away in her fancy sports car. It was hard to imagine what was going on with her that she was this upset about her ex-husband showing up in town. Silas would not tolerate him anywhere close to her, and that much Kellie knew, so that could be an interesting scenario too.

Silas was much older than Laura, and very controlling.

Kellie stepped inside and quickly filled in the booking

information for the reservation into her hard-bound journal at the front desk, then went to prepare dinner. Tonight it would be pasta and seafood. She hadn't even asked Jenner if he ate seafood, and now she worried if he were allergic or something. In the kitchen, she quickly worked, getting the pasta and the sauce just perfect. She had a big salad ready and garlic bread warming in the oven.

When the front door opened, she checked that everything was good for a moment, and then she raced out to the front. And, sure enough, there was Jenner. "Hey, you ready for food?"

He nodded. "Absolutely. Kinda hungry actually."

"The only thing is, I forgot to ask"—she stopped and gave him an apologetic look—"if you're okay with seafood? You noted no allergies or anything on your registration."

"I'm totally okay with seafood," he stated, looking at her curiously. "What's on the menu?"

"It's a pasta dish that I've been making for years. I got a hankering for it this morning," she explained, "so I guess that's what's for dinner."

"Sounds good to me." He stepped into the kitchen behind her and sniffed the air. "Perfectly okay with me. I'm always happy to have home-cooked food."

"There is something special about it, isn't there?" she asked, tossing him a bright smile.

He nodded. "Especially after a number of years of not getting it."

"I guess in the navy you end up not always eating the best food."

"There's always lots, and it's always filling," he noted, "but sometimes they completely miss the mark in terms of what you would like to eat and taste. They're not chefs, but they produce a lot of food very quickly."

"Got it. Do you want to sit in the dining room?"

"Where will you sit?" She hesitated, and then he asked, "Or do you want to eat on your own? Don't answer that." He flushed. "Sorry, I didn't mean to cross a line."

"And you didn't," she replied, and, from her perspective, it was nice of him to even consider that. She worked on finishing up dinner. "I just didn't want to push myself on you. Lots of my visitors prefer to eat privately."

"Not me. I've spent too much time alone," he stated. "I'm just grateful to have a home-cooked meal."

"Did you find the neighbors' place?" She turned to look at him.

He nodded. "I did, indeed. It was deserted. No sign of any dogs. Not sure that I saw anything in particular pointing to signs of dogs, but I was short on time so didn't dwell."

"Yeah, definitely to make it here for dinner while it's hot," she noted. "Plus, you may want to take a good look around first, just in case something odd is going on there."

He laughed. "You wouldn't be at all unhappy if there was, and I put a stop to it, *huh?*"

"I don't think he's doing anything illegal," she clarified, with a shrug. "He's just one of those guys who makes you nervous, if you walk down an alleyway."

"I do know," he stated, "and he certainly won't be bothering you while I'm here." She looked at him in surprise. He shrugged. "It's not in me to leave somebody alone to deal with somebody like that. However, chances are good though that he'll take one look at me and not give you any headaches, until I'm gone again."

"And that would be very typical of him too, I would think."

"Did I see a sports car leave here, as I walked back again?"

"Yeah, that's a friend of mine," she shared. "Laura's due with her first child, and her parents and family want to come visit for the birth of the child, but her husband won't let anybody stay with her." She wondered why he suddenly had gone very still.

He asked, "Laura?"

She nodded. "Yeah, we've been friends for about five years," she replied. "This is her second marriage."

"Interesting," he murmured.

"Why?"

"Because one of the things that I did when I knew I was coming here," he shared, "was to call my ex-wife, to let her know I would be in town, and I'd like to meet up with her."

She stared at him. "Oh my." Then she turned to plate the two servings.

His lips twitched. "That's an odd reaction."

"No," she murmured, but she wasn't sure what to say. To think that this was Laura's ex-husband? Then Kellie compared him to Silas and wondered what had gotten into Laura's head. "She did mention her ex."

"Mention what?"

"Just that her ex had phoned, and she seemed kind of rattled."

He stared at her. "Interesting. She's married, right?"

Kellie nodded and carried the plates to the dining room table. "Yeah, but she made some comment about she wasn't the person she was before, and she hadn't left things in a very good state."

He didn't say much at first and nodded. "Yeah, as far as I understood at the time, she was marrying my best friend."

"Oh, ouch," she replied in fascination. "Honestly, I don't know anything about it. Come and eat."

"And that's fine," he stated. "I'm not talking out of turn or expecting you to say anything. If she doesn't get hold of me, she doesn't get hold of me." He shrugged. "I just thought it might be an opportunity to mend some bridges."

"Well, she is married, and she is pregnant and, I believe, happy."

"Good." He nodded. "Nothing's between us anymore, and anything that was there is not something I care to rekindle. For me, trust is everything."

At that, Kellie had to wonder because it sounded like he couldn't trust Laura, which would also hurt. "I'm sorry. I'm sorry I ever mentioned it."

He laughed. "How could you know? I came here for the War Dog, but I figured, while I was in town, maybe I could mend some fences, but more for a sense of moving on and leaving it all behind. Not that I'm carrying any torches for her or anything," he stated. "It just occurred to me that maybe I was holding some grudges that I needed to let go of."

"That's always a good thing to deal with," she noted cautiously. "I'm not sure how receptive her husband will be if you see her."

"Obviously not very happy," he agreed, "and I initially had thought her husband was my best friend. Then I heard rumors it wasn't."

"Silas Kentrol," she shared.

He frowned at her. "She married Silas Kentrol?"

She nodded. "Do you know him too?"

"I do. He was a best friend of her father's, I believe."

"Yes, he's quite a bit older than she is."

He stared for a moment, then resumed eating. "This is a lovely dinner, by the way."

Something was odd about his voice. "Thank you," she murmured, while wondering how they had ended up in such a strange conversation and how he must feel to realize who Laura had ended up marrying. But it sounded like she had deliberately thrown Jenner off by saying she was with someone else. Kellie wasn't even sure what was going on in Laura's mind. Kellie had certainly been curious as to why this beautiful young woman had married somebody a lot older than she was.

When Jenner was done with his plateful, he smiled up at Kellie. "This was an absolutely wonderful meal. I really appreciate it."

And there was sincerity in his voice, enough that she realized he wasn't just making it up. "Good, I really love cooking," she murmured, "so a bed-and-breakfast seemed like a great idea at the time."

"But maybe not now?" he asked, with a quirk of his lips.

"Sometimes it is. Sometimes the conversations can get a little bit bizarre."

"Yes, it sure can, but you don't have to be a bed-and-breakfast if you don't want to do that. Surely other occupations interest you? What made you decide to get into this?"

"The house was my family's," she explained. "Then they moved to Europe, didn't want anything to do with it anymore. It was my grandparents' first. My parents inherited it from them. Then I bought the place off them, had a few hiccups getting started again, and here I am. It's a good way to make an income, along with the horses."

"You have horses too?"

"I think everybody here does," she admitted, "but I actually board horses, senior horses that are no longer being actively ridden. I just provide the place. The owners come out here and feed and water and brush them, so it's nice for everybody."

He looked at her with interest.

"Basically I just give them a nice home, so that they can live out the rest of their years. Some are actually charity on my part, and some are ones that I get paid to keep. The paid ones help cover the cost of the ones that I'm helping out along the way. I have a vet assistant who sees to those, feeding and watering them and whatever. So I pay her a little something to do that, as it helps me so much."

"Because horses are not cheap," he murmured and nodded.

"Exactly."

"My family used to live around here," he noted. "My mom was killed in a horse riding accident, and my father hated horses forevermore, and we ended up moving to California. When I got of age, I signed up with the navy, was stationed there when I met Laura, before I ever realized that she was from here. It was such a weird feeling to realize that she was part of Ashland that I had learned to hate because of my mother's death, but I only hated it because my father did. So, by the time I worked my way through all that crap," he added, "Laura and I spent a fair bit of time here."

"I'm not surprised. She has a lot of family nearby," Kellie replied, wondering how they ended up back on the Laura topic again.

He looked over at her and then chuckled. "I know. Honestly, I'm not fixated on her. I think it's just being back here again and dealing with the memories," he explained, as he got up, carrying his plate to the sink. "Where do you want me to wash the dishes?"

"Oh no you don't." She bounced to her feet. "You're not washing them."

He shook his head. "I don't mind."

"No, absolutely no way." And she quickly took the plate from his hands. "Go sit down for a few minutes. I'll get the dishes started and put on some coffee, if you would like." She turned around to glance at him.

He nodded. "I would really like a cup. I always appreciate a good cup, but right now? ... I'd love it."

"And I do have dessert."

"Okay, if you've got dessert"—he grinned—"I promise I'll go sit down, like a good boy."

She burst out laughing. "Sounds like dessert is what makes you sit up and pay attention."

"Absolutely. I've always had a bit of a sweet tooth. I just try to keep it under control."

"I've always done a whole lot of cooking, trying to keep the sugar mostly in control too," she murmured. "However, I do love to bake as well, so I generally have something sweet around."

"Well, I won't complain." He sat down at the kitchen table but then hopped up and immediately cleared her plates from the dining room table and brought them over.

"Stop, stop, stop," she fussed.

He shrugged. "I'm not used to just doing nothing."

"When you were injured, you were," she argued, "because you would have been in bed. So think back to being an invalid."

"Do I have to?" He groaned. "Those are years I would like to cheerfully forget."

"Did it take long to recover?"

"Maybe not," he murmured. "But I had three different surgeries, multiple skin grafts, and the list just goes on. It seems like it was years, but it was probably only about nine months, but you don't really ever forget that stage of your life."

He sat back down obediently and watched her. She quickly bustled around the kitchen, put on coffee, loaded the dishwasher, came back with a dishcloth, and quickly wiped the dining table.

He lifted a few things to help her wipe underneath them, and she asked, "So apple pie or cinnamon buns?"

He looked at her in shock. "You mean, I can have one or the other?"

"Sure," she replied. "I have both."

"Ah, well, that's a really hard decision."

"You can have one of each," she offered. "Did you get enough food to eat?"

"Oh, I'm fine," he said, "but, as you probably know, for anybody with a sweet tooth, there's always room in the back tummy for desserts."

At his term *back tummy*, her laughter rang out. "Oh my, you sound like a kid."

"When it comes to desserts, I'm a kid," he confirmed, with a big grin.

She walked over to the kitchen, brought out a dessert tray from a cupboard and carried it to the kitchen table. He studied the apple pie, as she went to the fridge and brought out something from there. She brought that over, so he could take a look at both.

"Cinnamon rolls with cream cheese icing. I don't mind if you want one of each," she repeated. "I mean, they certainly won't keep all that long."

"Absolutely. I really think I should take one for the team and help you out with that."

She nodded solemnly. "You know what? I think you're quite right." And she quickly dished him up a piece of apple pie and then, on a separate small plate, a cinnamon bun. He stared down at the two dishes, and she could almost see him rubbing his hands together. She grinned. "I don't know. You look way too happy right now."

"No such thing," he declared. "After years of military food, then hospital food, and then what little bit I could concoct myself, treats like these have only happened in restaurants."

"Oh, I guess you didn't have a partner to help you bake?"

"Nope, never did. Even when I did, she didn't cook."

And Kellie remembered that Laura didn't cook at all. Kellie nodded. "Well, in this case, I love to cook."

"And I love to eat, so it's a match made in heaven." With that, he reached for his fork and dug in.

JENNER WAS HAPPY to be back on a more normal and natural footing with Kellie because the conversations about his ex were something he did not in any way expect to share with her. They did make her uncomfortable, and he was sorry about that.

The cinnamon buns and apple pie in front of him after the meal that he'd just gulped down were a huge boon. She was absolutely a wonderful cook, and he knew he would thoroughly enjoy his time here. Even if, so far, he had no idea how to proceed on the War Dog's case.

He studied her covertly, as she bustled around the kitchen, cleaning up and washing pots and pans. She was trim, small, auburn-haired, nothing terribly gorgeous about her—like there had been about Laura—but he really appreciated a wholesomeness and a naturalness to Kellie. A quiet joy surrounded her, one he appreciated.

Her face was just so mobile that he found himself constantly watching her lips, wondering what it would be like to kiss them. He knew that she would be incredibly responsive. Yet here he was, having an awkward conversation that he had brought up about his ex-wife. He pondered his actions. What had him thinking that contacting Laura was a good thing in any way?

Maybe I shouldn't have.

Maybe it was better to let things be. He was absolutely stunned to hear that she was pregnant, and yet again that she was pregnant with Silas's child. And that was another stunner. Silas was at least twenty if not forty years older than her. Jenner just couldn't see the two of them together, couldn't comprehend the reason behind it at all. So thinking about *why* was beyond him.

Being here and knowing that she'd just been at the B&B, chances were good that Jenner would have no way to avoid Laura, even if he had chosen to.

It was just one more of those strange circumstances that brought him back here. Not exactly sure why but Jenner somehow knew that it would be good to walk away and to know that it was done and dealt with, as far as Laura goes. If just curiosity kept him mentally angry, then to resolve that would be a good thing.

He didn't want anything to do with Laura; obviously trust was something that he had struggled with at this point in time. Getting over that would help him to look at other relationships from a healthier viewpoint. Part of him wanted to understand why Laura left him. And with whom?

And yet he didn't know that getting those kinds of answers would help at all. Laura was somebody who wanted more in life, and obviously she felt Jenner couldn't get that for her. Silas, Jenner recalled, had been incredibly wealthy, and, with that realization, it almost made sense that she'd hook up with him. Money and prestige mattered to Laura. But, on the opposite side of that, she'd loved nightclubs and partying. He couldn't see that as Silas's lifestyle. And yet what she really loved, Jenner acknowledged, was what money could buy. So maybe it did make a lot of sense for her to marry Silas.

Jenner finally put down his fork and looked over at Kellie. "Thank you. That was delicious."

She flashed him a bright smile. "Good."

The word was said in such a natural way that he knew she was just being herself again.

"I'm really glad that you enjoyed it."

He got up, walked over, and handed her the dishes.

"Breakfast is at eight, if that's okay." She looked over at him. "Unless you're an early riser?"

He thought about it. "I am an early riser. I'm not sure what tomorrow will bring though," he murmured.

"Well, if you want anything earlier," she offered, "let me know. I am up early every morning."

When he looked at her curiously, she added, "I go to bed early, and I get up early." She shrugged. "So, if you're up at six or seven, that's fine. Coffee would be on as soon as I get up."

"Perfect." He nodded and stepped away.

He headed up to his room, where he pulled out his laptop. What he hadn't told her was the property several houses down where the dogs were supposed to be had looked empty and deserted. He wasn't sure what that was all about, when, according to her, dogs had been there just a few weeks ago. He would go there again this evening for another walk and see what he could come up with. It made sense that the War Dog was now possibly in trouble or had been sold to another family, if the son were now in charge of Sisco. Except, if the son already had multiple dogs, there was no reason not to keep that one in particular.

Jenner quickly phoned Badger and gave him an update.

"Have you met up with your wife?"

"My ex-wife and no. She's married to somebody who's decades older than her," he shared, and, although uncomfortable, he had to get it off his chest. "Apparently she's pregnant."

"And how do you feel about that?" Badger asked curiously.

"Glad it's not me," he noted bluntly. "I forgot how much money meant to her, so it makes sense in a way that she has married somebody so much older. He was very wealthy."

"Maybe she had an insecurity about being destitute," Badger replied. "Still, it's her problem."

"That's how I feel," Jenner agreed. "I'll head down to the neighbor's house again and take a walk around and see what I come up with tonight. According to the bed-and-breakfast owner, the son had multiple dogs, but today I didn't hear or see any signs or sounds of any dogs."

"Okay," Badger murmured.

"She also has problems with the owner now, the son, in

the sense that he's somebody she feels threatened by and who pushes her personal space boundaries and comes drunk after hours to the bed-and-breakfast, at times that she's not comfortable with."

"Interesting, so maybe give him a good side-eye, see what else he has got going on there."

"That's what I thought," Jenner agreed. "If nothing else, I need to find out why it looked completely deserted earlier today."

"And not to mention nobody should know that you're there," Badger noted.

"No, nobody should know, and nobody should know what I'm after is the War Dog, so no reason for this guy to have bolted."

"Well, go take a look," Badger said. "See what kind of problems you've got happening down there."

"Does it always happen with problems?"

"Yeah," he admitted. "Seems like there's always a problem. Sometimes it's relatively easy to solve, but, so far, we haven't found very many easy ones along the way."

"Of course not," Jenner replied. "I'm up for whatever. I'd like to find Sisco though."

And, with that, he hung up, walked down the stairs carefully, hopped back up a few risers, and went down again, checking on that joint. When he looked up, Kellie stared at him. He smiled. "Just checking to see if I needed to borrow the Allen wrench again."

She burst out laughing. "Doesn't look like you suffer too much from it," she stated, with a note of admiration. "Honestly, I didn't even know, until you lifted your pant leg."

"That's the way it should be," he stated. "I've been

working with a friend of mine. She designs these prosthetics, so I tend to wear a bunch of her prototypes and give them a good old tryout. If nothing else, I can put them through the hard wear and tear to see how they size up."

"Fascinating," she replied. "Are you an engineer?"

"No, not necessarily," he said, "but I am a tech, so I do a lot of modeling online, and then we build prototypes, and I get to play them up."

"Sounds wonderful to me."

He lifted a hand and waved. "I'll just head back down to take another look."

She nodded. "Good enough, but remember I lock up at ten."

"And if I'm later?"

She winced. "Well, hopefully you won't be too much later, but it's a typical bed-and-breakfast. I lock up for last time at eleven, but I prefer to lock up at ten."

"Got it. I'll try to be back by ten. If not, how about I call you?"

"Do that, please." She gave him a grateful nod. "I hate locking up if everybody isn't tucked up in their beds."

He grinned at her. "I bet you'd make a great Santa Claus." With that, he walked out and down to the house in question. As he wandered along the roadside, he saw nothing but lots of barns.

The house he wanted to check was blanketed in darkness; no vehicles were parked out front. The residence showed some disrepair, and yet, if the family hadn't been gone for more than two months, it shouldn't be showing this much, unless they'd had been living here under pretty rough conditions already.

He walked up to the front door and knocked. When no

answer came, he called out, "Hello, hello."

Still, there was no answer. Frowning, he walked down the full length of the big long veranda and looked in the windows. He saw absolutely no furniture, nothing. Frowning at that, he headed around to the back of the house, wondering if the guy had just gotten up in the middle of the night and had disappeared.

As Jenner walked around to the side of the house, he heard a faint cry. He followed the sound, calling out, "Hello," and then came another faint cry. He followed it farther into the field and found a man crumpled on his back, down in a ditch. Jenner immediately raced to his side. "Hey."

"Oh thank God," the man cried out.

"Jesus. Are you okay?"

"No, I'm not okay." He groaned. "I hate to say it, but I need an ambulance."

Jenner noted that one leg was bent underneath him at an odd angle, but, even more so, he was missing the other leg. "Hang on," he told him. "I'll get you an ambulance. I would pick you up and move you, but I'm afraid about that leg."

"I've been through so much already," the other man said, gasping in pain. "Just get the ambulance. I don't want to lose the other leg."

"Got it," he said. "I've got a prosthetic myself, so I understand."

The guy looked at Jenner and then groaned again. "Jesus, the pain."

"Can you tell me what happened?" Jenner asked, as he quickly put through the phone call. With that done, he looked at the other man. When he didn't answer his question, Jenner asked again quite forcefully. "Can you tell me what happened?"

"I came over here to look at my parents' place," he replied. "I hadn't been here for a while. I was in surgery, trying to get the leg fixed, but it's been a rough couple months since my parents died." He gasped at the pain again. "There was ... some guy here, with a whole pile of dogs. I was supposed to come here and look after and take care of the place, but the surgeries held me back."

"You are the son?" Jenner asked.

The guy looked at him and said, "Yeah. My parents owned this place since forever. I was raised in this house. But some asshole was living here, and, when I confronted him about it, we ended up in a hell of a fight, which I, of course, completely lost. It was stupid. Emotions got the better of me, but he knocked me out. What I should have done was to just bring in the cops and have him arrested."

"I'm sorry to hear that," Jenner muttered. "I'm staying at the B&B up the road. She thought the other guy was the son though."

"I haven't been here in years," he explained. "I don't really have a whole lot to do with this place, since I went into the military and got injured. Now I was hoping to come home and to look after it and to have a place for me that maybe, if I could get it wheelchair accessible, ... I could actually live here again. It is mine, but this squatter took over the place, and then he dumped me in the back here."

"And it looks like he's buggered off too."

"Good," he muttered, "although I would sure as hell like to know what the heck he was doing here."

"I gather he's been here for quite a few weeks too."

The guy stared at him in shock. "Jesus. I sure as hell hope he didn't cause any damage, and, if he's gone now, that's great."

"I looked in the living room window, and it looks like all the big pieces have been cleaned out. Saw some papers on the floor. Don't know whether that was wrapping paper to move the stuff or some documents. How long have you been here in the ditch?"

He shook his head. "I don't know. Overnight for sure."

"Jesus, well, I'm glad I found you now."

"I tried to drag myself forward," he noted, "then I kind of slid into the ditch. The damn leg."

"Hey, don't worry about it. You'll be fine now," Jenner told him.

"The squatter might have been moving out already," he guessed. "I don't know. When I saw him, he had a big truck here."

Jenner nodded. "It looks to be cleaned out right now. Let's get you fixed up, and then we can sort it out." He asked him gently, "So your parents?"

The guy nodded. "Yeah"—gasping in agony—"what about them?"

"I understand that they died in a car accident."

"Yes," he confirmed, "that's what I just said."

"Right, and they had a War Dog, didn't they?"

The guy looked at Jenner and then nodded slowly. "Yeah, they did. Why?"

"Because I'm here on behalf of the war department, wondering what happened to the dog. Somebody did a welfare check, and there was a problem."

"Yeah, my parents died," he snapped, "but I'm not even sure what happened to the dog."

"Apparently the bed-and-breakfast owner, Kellie, didn't see one like it around."

"It may have taken off on its own, without my parents here. Maybe one of the neighbors stole it. I don't know what happened, but I'll find out. I am so sorry. I didn't realize that they had any animals left to even look after, and I was caught up in the hospital, so I wasn't exactly doing much about it. The sheriff did say that he didn't see any animals on the premises."

"Interesting," Jenner murmured.

"Right," the son noted. "Honestly, I have no clue. One more thing to get to the bottom of, while wondering if I can get back on my feet."

In the distance Jenner heard the sirens. "Or first off, you need to look after you. Once I point the EMTs in your direction, I'll take a look around, see if the War Dog's here, if you don't mind."

"Yeah, please do." He hesitated and then added, "I don't know if you've got a few minutes, but could you do an inventory, let me know if there's anything to come home to?"

"Sure will. At least I'll go in and take some photos." He quickly got the guy's phone number, so he could tag him later. "Let's get you taken care of first." With that, he raced to the driveway, directed the ambulance to the back, where they came and found him. Jenner asked the son, "What's your name?"

"Jim. Call the sheriff too, will you?"

"Will do," Jenner replied. "Where's your phone?"

"No clue. I think I lost it on the ground, where I started dragging myself, and I didn't have the energy to get back there."

"I'll go take a look." Following Jim's rough directions, even as the ambulance drove closer to Jim, Jenner found the phone by ringing it with his own. It had been left out in the elements, but it was still here. He raced back to the ambulance and handed it to him. "At least now you have a phone."

"Great, I'll call the sheriff myself."

"You do that, and I'll contact you after I've been through the house."

And, with that, Jenner watched as the ambulance took off. He headed back to Jim's house and took various photos. As he got into the front door, he stopped and swore. It's not that too much damage had been done by the squatter or just by the passage of time and not enough money to fix things, but, whatever had been here of the family's, it was long gone. Furniture was all gone. Some of the floorboards were scratched, as if not much care had been taken when dragging out the heavier pieces.

Jenner figured this squatter had just decided, with Jim's sudden appearance, that he would lose the place, so he might as well just take what he wanted, and that was certainly possible here. Or it sounded like the squatter had already been in the process of moving to begin with. Jenner wandered through, took a bunch of photos, knowing that, if there had been family heirlooms here, they were long gone too.

Upstairs it was the same story; the place had been cleaned out thoroughly. He presumed there would have been probably decent sturdy stuff here but not likely too high-end. The house itself was old but nice enough, very much a country family home. It would be devastating for Jim to restock everything, but it could be so much worse. This squatting asshole could have come in and burned the place to the ground.

It didn't explain where the War Dog was. As soon as Jenner was done, he walked downstairs, needing to check the kitchen, but headed outside and inspected all the outbuildings, before it got too dark. When he was finished with that, he heard a vehicle coming up to the front door of the house. It was getting dark out, and, as Jenner headed to the front yard, he saw the vehicle marked with the sheriff's symbol on the side panel. Jenner walked over and introduced himself.

"You're the guy who found Jim," the sheriff noted, reaching out and shaking his hand.

"Yeah, and I told him that I'd send him some photos of his place because Jim thought the squatter has been cleaning it out. I am sorry to say, but nothing is left in there."

The sheriff swore at that. "What the hell is the world coming to that they clean out the house after the family's been killed off?"

"So sorry about that," Jenner noted. "I'm looking for the War Dog that the family had." At that, the sheriff looked at him. "Did you know about it?"

"I did, indeed," the sheriff confirmed. "I figured the dog just took off or maybe the parents made other arrangements, but it wasn't here when I came and checked on the property. After a death like that, it's an automatic welfare check, looking to see what animals need to be taken care of, but no dog was here."

"That's a hell of a mystery," Jenner replied, looking around. "Jim didn't seem to know anything about it either."

"No, Jim's had a pretty rough couple years. He's been in and out of surgeries constantly. He was in a coma for a while. We didn't think he would make it. I know the parents were absolutely ecstatic when he pulled back out. He was getting rehabbed and back on his feet again. But, while he had been in the coma, one of his legs didn't work properly, and he lost it," the sheriff explained, with a headshake. "I think they were actually on their way home from the hospital when they died."

"Ouch, that's a double whammy for Jim too."

"Exactly, but this?" The sheriff motioned at the house, as he walked up to the front door. "This is just disgusting. To think somebody would come in here and just strip it clean."

"And I think the squatter had been living here for a while," he related.

At that, the sheriff spun to look at him. "What?"

"If you talk to Kellie at the bed-and-breakfast, she told me how his dogs circled her to the point that she was terrified to move, and, if the dogs' owner hadn't been there, she didn't think that the dogs would have been called off. She pretty well thought that the dogs would kill her."

He swore. "Why didn't she say something?"

"I'm not sure," Jenner replied. "I get the impression that she didn't know what to do, but the dog's owner scared her really badly too."

"Well, that wouldn't have been Jim."

"I gather she didn't know Jim and that she was speaking of the squatter," he noted.

"No, not too many people have seen Jim around recently. It's been quite a few years since he was back home. He was supposed to come home, but all of this blew up."

"I'm sorry for Kellie's sake, and I'm sorry she didn't mention it to anybody."

"She should have at least let me know about the damn dogs," the sheriff complained. "I can't have that happening, and maybe that's what moved the squatter out. Maybe he figured, after that incident with her, he had better start looking for another place." He nodded. "I'll give her a ring and see what she's got to add." He looked back over at Jenner. "What will you do now?"

"I need to find the War Dog," Jenner stated. "I'm out here on behalf of the War department. I won't walk away without getting something."

The sheriff frowned at that and kicked a couple rocks. "The parents didn't have any problems with that dog. There was no reason for it not to be here," he explained. "Honestly, I did come back soon after their deaths. I was here a few times that week, but, when I found no dog, there just wasn't any reason to return. I was waiting for Jim to get back here instead."

"Do you know if the parents might have sent the dog to a temporary home to be cared for? Did they have any friends who raised animals, anything like that?"

"No, and they loved that dog," the sheriff confirmed. "All I can think about was that it took off."

"It might have taken off if the squatter had come in and obviously a well-disciplined War Dog would have some issues with the squatter's aggressive dogs. That War Dog's got a damaged ankle or two, and he is trained to defend himself and others, but he would be looking for people who actually protected him too. He wouldn't have expected to be attacked."

"I hate to say it, but it's quite possible that I just didn't see it here. I know that the Stippletones had some issues with the dog wanting to be left alone. So maybe it just didn't want to come to me because it didn't recognize me. Then, when the squatter moved in, the dog may have just decided to take off, rather than get attacked."

"So this squatter could have moved in right after the

parents died a couple months ago, but we know for sure, from Kellie, that the guy's been there for a few weeks," Jenner muttered, looking at the sheriff intently.

He shrugged. "I don't know what to tell you."

It's obvious that the sheriff didn't know anything and was getting tired of having anything even brought up along that line. Jenner nodded. "I'll keep looking around. Maybe the War Dog's loose in the countryside."

"If that were the case, I should have heard about it," the sheriff replied. "People don't take kindly to wild dogs on the run here. Everybody's got horses, and people are pretty protective about their livestock."

"The War Dog wouldn't hurt livestock …" Then Jenner stopped. "No, I can't say that. The dog's got to eat."

CHAPTER 3

THE NEXT MORNING Kellie got up bright and early, wondering if she should phone the sheriff's office, since seeing him go down the road, along with the ambulance last night. She had only stayed up long enough for her boarder to return so she could lock up, and he had just raced upstairs. So she hadn't gotten any answers from him. She wanted to ask but there hadn't been any update online in the news either. She made coffee and set about putting sausages on. When the coffee was done, she turned down the sausages and settled on the back porch with a cup, leaving the rear door to the kitchen open.

Hearing movement inside, she called out, "Coffee's in the kitchen."

"Got it." He hesitated at her back door, even though open.

"Hey, you're welcome to come out."

"Thank you," he replied, "I'm always very mindful when in somebody else's house."

"I think I gave up a lot of that privacy when I turned it into a bed-and-breakfast, but I happen to like people, so it works."

"I'm glad for you. It's not something that everybody would be comfortable doing."

She nodded. "So can I ask a question?"

"Sure. What's up?"

"Last night," she noted, "I heard the ambulance, and I thought I saw the sheriff's vehicle." He nodded and quickly told her what he had found, when he went back down to Jim's house. She stared at him, her jaw dropping. "Good Lord." She tried to assimilate the news. It was heartbreaking. "So, not only is the man I've been dealing with not the son," she said, "but the real son, who came to check on his parents' place, was beaten up, and he's injured?"

"He is missing a leg, like I am," he confirmed, with a kick of his bad leg. "Anyway I went through the homestead, took a bunch of photos for Jim, and I talked with the sheriff briefly. He was asking to talk to you about your altercations with this man."

She gulped. "Wow. Now if only I had called him at the time. But I was determined to avoid any kind of issues, so I just kept quiet."

"And the problem with keeping quiet is then you never really know if it was something that needed to be reported," he murmured.

"Yes, exactly." She raised both her hands, palms up. "I just didn't even think that something like that was possible. That poor man."

"You and a lot of other people, I'm sure," he murmured. "So you've never met Jim?"

"No." She shook her head. "I've spoken to his parents a lot, but I've only been back here myself for the last three odd years. I lived here a long time ago, of course, since it's my family's estate, but I only bought it from them somewhat recently. It stood empty for a couple years, while they traveled and decided what they would do, and while I figured out how to run this place," she explained.

"Ah, got it. I assumed that you've been here for the last decade plus."

"No, no, not at all," she replied. "Just how weird is that though?"

"Right? Anyway, expect a phone call from the sheriff today."

She winced at that. "He's not exactly one of my favorite people."

"Are the police anybody's favorite people?" he asked, with a cheeky grin.

She smiled. "I guess for some people. For me though, I always feel like I've done something wrong when I talk to him."

"Even though you haven't done anything and probably never have in your entire life."

She immediately nodded. "Yeah, just something about authority figures and I want to blurt out and confess to absolutely everything"—she laughed nervously—"when, in fact, I haven't ever done anything criminal in my life to confess to. I'm sure my type of reaction is unusual."

"No, actually it's quite usual," Jenner noted.

She chuckled. "So how will you track down the dog then?"

"That's the next challenge I have." He frowned. "I'll check around and see if anybody has seen anything like it. I don't know if there are any rescues in the area, but I'll check them too. Maybe the dog found its own way to somebody else."

"*Hmm.* A bunch of rescues are in town. I do know one that, if I had an animal in need to go someplace, I would definitely send it to them. Susan is very compassionate."

"If you have a contact number, I'll call her as soon as I've had breakfast. Then I'll head down and talk to her."

"Sure. She's certainly got lots of people she works with to help resettle animals, depending on the circumstances. She's got a heart of gold."

"And those are the kind of people these animals need." Jenner sipped his coffee. "No judgments, just acceptance."

"Hey, that's the kind of people we *all* need," she murmured.

He looked over at her curiously.

"I'm not immune to a lot of the gossip and the fearmongering that people do in small towns." She shrugged. "I haven't been in this particular area for a while, but I did grow up here, and I suffered an awful lot of judgment."

"Any hidden tales in there that I should be aware of?"

She shook her head. "No, but what I can tell you is that most of the people here have very long memories."

"Ah, and that goes back to my ex-wife again, I presume." Kellie nodded. "I would hate to come between you."

"Oh, you can't come between us," he stated. "There is no *us*. I'd hate to come between the two of you."

She shrugged. "Laura is a friend, but obviously we live in different spheres, and I don't even know if we are good friends. I mean, ... I run a bed-and-breakfast, and she's the lady in town."

He burst out laughing at that. "I could say a lot about that, but I won't."

She nodded because she pretty well could have read his lips, saying that she's not a lady. Kellie had often wondered about the very strange relationship between Laura and Silas, but Kellie had decided not to say anything either way.

"Anyway, as soon as I've had breakfast ..."

At that, she hopped to her feet. "Right, you've mentioned that a couple times now. I have sausages warming. I would suggest toast and eggs, unless you're in need of something more substantial, like pancakes?"

"Why? You're the one who said it was a continental breakfast."

She shrugged. "I lied. I say that so I have some flexibility with my cooking."

He burst out laughing. "You'll never make a profit doing that."

"No, but I enjoy my job, and I have fun doing it, and that's got to be worth something." Leaving him sitting alone on the back porch, she walked into the kitchen, knowing that her comment had surprised him. But then she was a little bit of a free spirit, and that attitude had gotten her into a lot of trouble when she was younger.

While she had helped off and on in the family's B&B when her family ran it, she took over the bed-and-breakfast as the solo cook and bottle washer. Her parents had really hesitated because they were afraid that she didn't have any business sense and wouldn't be able to handle it. It's not that she didn't have *any* business sense. It's just that, if somebody were in need, Kellie was right there for them, and that got her in more trouble than her parents liked to see. She heard the rear door close behind her, and she turned to see Jenner walking toward the kitchen table. "Help yourself to a second cup of coffee too," she said. "I really don't hold anybody to limits."

He nodded. "Thanks. It's nice to know that I don't have to worry about it."

"Not with me," she stated. "An awful lot in life is worth worrying about, but something like that is not."

"And I like that attitude too," he admitted. "You've certainly got me curious with your comment about long memories."

She winced. "Oh, I wasn't trying to make you curious by any means." She chuckled. "Just, you know, when you all grow up in one town, it seems like everybody already has a very long memory of things that you may or may not have done that they didn't agree with."

"Ah, isn't that the truth? Unfortunately it happens way more often than we think, doesn't it?"

She nodded. "It just seems like somebody always remembers when you were thirteen years old, and you were papering the neighborhood with other locals."

He looked at her and then chuckled. "On Halloween night, by any chance?"

She nodded. "Absolutely."

"I think those are just like rites of passage when you're a kid, you know? You get to throw all those rules and regulations out the window and hope you don't get in trouble too badly."

She snorted. "Then there's the fact that I was supposed to go to the prom with my boyfriend at the time, but he ended up going with the most popular girl, who was my best friend, who *wasn't* his girlfriend at the time," she explained, with a head shake. "*That was not fun.*"

"Ouch, that's like public humiliation number one for a teenager."

"Right? Apparently he didn't seem to care, and neither did she. He also didn't bother breaking up with me first."

He stared at her. "Wow, nice guy."

"Nope, not at all. Of course lots of pitying glances followed all that for a very long time," she added.

"It takes a while to live some of that down."

"Some of it you just never get a chance to live down because people bring it up every time. Now thankfully most of that is long gone," she noted. "Unfortunately the boyfriend in question ended up getting arrested for drunk driving, and then, of course, that lovely girlfriend who was the most popular girl at the time ended up pregnant with somebody else's kid and took off. Never seen her since. Bad for them but took me out of the spotlight."

He just stared at her and then he started to laugh. "Yeah, sounds like a very small-town tale."

She nodded. "Yeah, sure does." And then she asked, "Two eggs or three?"

"Two and thank you," he replied. "Sounds like life here was never boring."

"Never boring, always dull."

"Ah." He nodded. "That's the other side of the coin, isn't it?"

He sat down at the table, and she brought over toast that had just popped, handed him a knife and butter, and added, "I think you can probably do this by yourself."

He chuckled. "Yes, and I absolutely can also help with other things, if you need it."

"No, sounds like you already don't know how to cook, so I'll handle that just fine."

"It's not so much that I don't know how to cook," he explained, "I just never managed to handle the timing. You know there's always so many things that have to be done all at once. Otherwise it all ends up cooked at different time periods, and none of it is warm by the time it hits the table."

She nodded. "That's just one of those little tricks that you have to learn, and it comes with practice."

"That's the part that I never did get," he muttered. "And

I really admire anybody who can make that happen at the same time."

She chuckled. "I think you'll just admire anybody who feeds you."

"Wow." He laughed out loud. "Is that fair? I mean, like really? Is that fair? I'm a nice guy. I'm quite happy to pass out the compliments, as long as you're feeding me."

Now she burst out laughing. "And I'm not sure if that will make things any better."

He grinned at her. "Hey, you never know. You might give me an extra sausage." And, for that, she promptly put another two on his plate. He looked at her and then at his plate and immediately frowned.

"Now you see? If you'll finagle your way into getting more food," she explained, "you can't just immediately look at your plate and frown. Because then I'll start to worry that I haven't given you enough." His glance immediately shot up, as he looked at her, and she nodded. "Yeah, I'm already figuring out who you are."

With that note of humor to ease some of the problems that they knew were coming later today, they both sat down to a good breakfast.

JENNER WALKED OUT of the bed-and-breakfast with two thoughts in his mind. One, he would have to walk the area behind Jim's house. It'd been two months since his parents' deaths, and the sheriff had stopped in to see about any animals left behind. And, sometime in that two-month period, the squatter had moved in with several dogs and had threatened Kellie at the bed-and-breakfast.

Two, Jenner also needed to stop at the hospital to talk to Jim. And, with everything cleaned out of his house, nothing of his parents remained there, but Jenner would go and take a closer look in drawers and closets and the attic even to see if any paperwork or something might have been missed.

Presumably somebody was working at shutting down bank accounts and things like that, but that wasn't Jenner's problem. There would be other people to handle that. It was more of Jenner's problem where Sisco went. And the longer this went on, the harder it was for the War Dog and for Jenner.

He walked down to the corner of the property, stopped and studied it, looking to see if anything was along the fence line to be seen, and of course there wasn't. That would be way too simple. Would have been nice if there were cameras everywhere you needed them, and they could catch all the criminals at the same time. *Not going to happen.*

He studied the sky, feeling a warm contentment; it was a warm day and still early in the morning, not even eight yet. As he walked across Jim's property, he crisscrossed it, looking for anything that might give him some answers. Not seeing anything here, he headed to the back of the property, where he'd found Jim. He studied the area, seeing where the man had dragged himself from and followed the tracks back.

It was hard to miss the signs of their altercation and where Jim had lain, probably unconscious. Tracks mingled around that were from dogs, and Jenner saw at least three to four different sets of prints. He frowned, as he headed back to the house. He let himself in through the back kitchen door and stood here, surveying the kitchen.

Almost everything here had been left intact, probably because the squatter didn't want to take anything from here.

Too many pieces to bother moving, probably breaking during the transfer. Jenner opened the fridge and saw groceries, a steak, some peanut butter, some bread, eggs, just a few basic necessities, not a vegetable in sight. He checked the cupboards, and they were definitely stocked, and food was abundant. Yet the squatter hadn't been interested in taking any of that.

There were also dishes, pots and pans, and essentials for cooking. Either there was no money in selling this stuff or the squatter already had another furnished spot picked out— or he was stopped before he had a chance to do more damage. He probably wondered if it was worth coming back here for this kitchen stuff, maybe even decided that it was definitely too dangerous to return to the scene of his crimes.

Jenner wandered through the house, looking at anything left in the garbage, on the floor, on the walls, anything that would indicate where the dog may have been, what happened, who the squatter was, even Jim's family mementos, but found nothing. Definitely crumpled brown wrapping paper was on the floor, but he didn't see anything important that stood out in particular.

He wandered through the house upstairs and down, and then headed back out the kitchen door to the back of the property. He hopped over the fence and kept walking.

He definitely saw holes in the fence, and the War Dog could have come and gone at any point in time. The fence was only four feet tall, and Sisco could have jumped that in a heartbeat, even with a bad ankle. Jenner wandered up the rise behind it and stopped where he could get a view. Lots of properties were all the way around.

He would have to knock on each one of those doors and see if anybody had seen the dog. For all he knew, somebody else was just feeding it and taking care of it. Maybe potentially even informally adopted it.

He headed down the far side to what looked like a more residential area, finding three to four houses on the end of a cul-de-sac. Making his way through to the front, he knocked on each of the doors, hoping that somebody would be home. As the people answered his questions, they looked at him with an odd look.

"What's the matter?" Jenner at last asked the third person, who stared him down pretty well. Jenner had to get to know these people to get the information that he needed, so it was important to establish a rapport.

"Well, it's awfully early in the morning to be wandering around, asking about a dog."

Jenner shrugged. "The dog's been on its own for too many weeks now."

"Exactly," she said in exasperation. "Why weren't you here when the dog went missing?"

"If we'd known about it," Jenner told her, "we would have been here, but nobody informed us."

She pondered that and then nodded. "I guess, just because you're a big bureaucracy, it doesn't mean you can read minds three hundred miles away, can you?" She then cackled at her own joke.

He gave her a smirk. "No, ma'am. If you do see the dog, please let me know." And he handed her a card.

He repeated the process with every person on that street. Nobody had seen the War Dog. Nobody knew anything about the stranger in Jim's house, and they were all very sympathetic over the death of the neighbors, who were known to most of them, having spent a lot of years here.

With that very frustrating and completely futile process,

Jenner headed back over the hill to the opposite side, where he was looking for any of the other properties that bordered Jim's. There were two, both with large acreages.

One man leaned against the doorjamb and glared at him.

Jenner took a step back, giving him some space. "We're just trying to find a War Dog," he explained.

"Maybe I shot it," he replied, with a shrug. "Shot a couple of them here lately. Nothing but trouble."

"How long ago?" he asked, thinking about what Sisco could have had been through, if he had been shot.

"About a month ago," he stated. "One was just bad news, came at me, sneering and hissing, ready to take my leg off. I popped him. Nobody really takes kindly to having dogs like that on the loose. I wasn't sure whose dog it was, and believe me. I didn't ask I just up and shot it."

"Do you know what it looked like?"

"Dark," he said, with a shrug.

"Small, black, like a shepherd?" Jenner asked, his heart in his throat.

The other man shook his head. "Hell no, not like a shepherd. Like a black Lab, although it was crossed with something else, maybe a Rottie." He shrugged. "Don't know."

"And the other one you shot?"

"It took off. I didn't get a second shot at it, and it hasn't come back. I think I shot its rump. Probably dead by now."

The other man had nothing else to offer, just that the two wild dogs had come after him, and he'd done what he could to defend himself. As Jenner wandered away, he muttered to himself, "So now we likely have one dead dog and a shot injured animal out there in the bush."

And nobody around here would argue with that guy's right to do that; it's just too bad that he didn't finish the job, and instead he had left a dangerous dog out here, now suffering. Of course Jenner didn't know how badly it was suffering or if it was even suffering.

Chances were good though that it would have been one of the bad bunch of dogs from the squatter that had circled and surrounded Kellie. That wasn't good either. But at least this man had the means to defend himself. As Jenner wandered up and around the other property, he found one other person who had something to say.

"Those dogs are bad news," he stated.

"But the dogs that were there are not the same when the owners were alive," Jenner tried to explain. "These were not the same pack but rather those of the squatter's."

"Maybe not," the neighbor replied, "but, around here, nobody'll give a shit. That dog you are looking for? He'll get shot the minute anybody sees him."

"Does everybody own guns around here?"

"Most of us have varmints," he explained. "Expensive horse flesh is in this area. Most people would do anything to look after their animals."

"Yeah, got it," Jenner replied. "However, if you do see a dark male shepherd, maybe you can give me a call?"

"You mean, after I shoot it or before?" he asked in a laconic tone.

Jenner winced at that. "*Before* would be very good."

"*Uh-huh*, not like the government ever did anything for me."

"No, but they're just trying to save an animal who did go to war for you," Jenner noted.

The other man shrugged. "War sucks, not my deal at

all."

"I get that too," he admitted, "but some people still feel very strongly about military veterans and War Dogs."

"You're just hoping that I do," he said, with a hard laugh. "Most of the time I don't give a shit about anything." With that, he walked back inside and slammed the door.

Not sure what else to do, Jenner headed back out, marked off the address on his map, and noted he'd missed a couple in this general location, but a dog like Sisco could have traveled to all kinds of places.

With a last glance at the area, Jenner walked back to the bed-and-breakfast, checking his watch. As he walked in the front door, Kellie looked up. "Hey. Any luck?"

He shook his head. "No, a few of the neighbors aren't the nicest bunch, and somebody did shoot a couple dogs here last month," he shared. "I'm wondering if they weren't the dogs that were after you."

She winced at that. "I don't know. As much as I don't agree with shooting an animal, there are times when personal safety does have to come into play."

"Absolutely," Jenner agreed. "It wasn't the War Dog in particular that I'm looking for, but I'm thinking it might have been those meaner ones with the squatter."

"I won't lose any sleep over it," she noted, "although the owner should take responsibility for those poor animals."

Jenner didn't say a whole lot, headed to his room, and came back down with his laptop. "Do you mind if I use the dining room table?"

She waved a hand. "Go ahead. It's all yours."

"And when do you have somebody coming in?"

"Not for a couple days yet," she replied. "Today's Monday. They'll be coming on Friday afternoon, as far as the last update goes."

"Have you heard from Laura?"

"Yeah." She looked over at him, surprised, and then slowly, as if not sure what to say, she shook her head.

He nodded. "You tell her whatever you feel comfortable telling her. You certainly don't have to hide my presence or run and tell her."

She gave him a one-arm shrug. "She's not that good a friend. She probably sees me as a vendor. I've been in town a lot longer, where I understand the nuances of those who have money and those who don't have any."

"She's now one with money, I presume."

"She always was," she replied, looking at him.

He shook his head. "Not when we were married. We didn't have any money."

"Interesting," she murmured. "I always assumed that she was part of that wealthy belt."

"Her family had money, but she didn't. I didn't."

"Well, she has it now," Kellie noted cheerfully, "and, as long as some of it comes my way in the form of good business, I'll do what I can to keep the peace."

"Absolutely." He turned back toward his laptop. Yet he was wondering what the hell kind of money Laura had actually married into. And then told himself to knock it off. It didn't matter. It was old history, and he was better off not knowing. He started updating Badger.

CHAPTER 4

KELLIE WATCHED AS Jenner worked for a few minutes, wondering how absolutely strange it must be to be in the same town as Laura, but Kellie also didn't know if he had any leftover feelings for his ex-wife. He had told Kellie that he didn't, and that it was all good, but she also knew that sometimes … those feelings played differently.

Kellie's parents had had some marital troubles at one point in time; she knew that her mother had stepped out on her father. It caused all kinds of hell, but they'd worked their way through it, and now they were over in England, together, doing whatever they did there. *Two peas in a pod.*

She shrugged. It didn't really matter to her, but, at the same time, those things never quite left you. She hated to think of her mother cheating on her father; surely her mother could have found some other way to deal with strife in her life other than to turn around and stick it to her father as hard as she could.

Kellie turned toward Jenner and said, "I'll be making some lunch. Do you want a bite?"

He looked up and frowned. "No, I know it's not included, but thank you for the offer."

"A sandwich won't kill me," she argued. "Besides, you're trying to find a dog. I'll never have a hard time helping somebody do that."

He gave her a bright smile that actually made her stop and stare.

"Wow, when you turn that smile on people, it's a dangerous weapon."

He looked at her, startled, his smile falling away.

She laughed. "That's more normal."

"Do I always look grumpy?" he asked gently.

"No, but that was a real smile, and I realized that it packed quite a punch."

"Anybody who loves animals," he noted, "is somebody I can get along with."

"Right. Too bad not enough people in this world do it all the time," she said. "It breaks my heart to even think of an animal suffering."

"Yours and mine both," he agreed.

"So I'll say, *Thank you very much* now and will go put lunch together. It'll be ready in a few minutes."

"Okay, just let me know." And he dropped his head back down to his work.

She wondered what he was supposed to do when he did find the dog. It's not like he was a local anymore. Where was he from? And would he go back there?

It took a special person to ensure the animal was set up properly. She had room for a dog, but that didn't mean that she was in any way willing to take on what sounded like a horrific responsibility when taking care of a War Dog. But then what did she know? She was all alone, and sometimes being all alone got damn lonely. Maybe the right dog would help her in that regard. Plus a War Dog would be a wonderful protector, she figured. Yet she had to consider her B&B guests. What if they were afraid of dogs or allergic or had small children and didn't want them hurt by bigger dogs?

She could do other things in life that would have the same impact in terms of not being lonely all the time—like joining a hiking club or a knitting or quilting group or a weekly card game or something, but she didn't really want to push it by getting a pet that was a huge commitment like that.

In the kitchen, she quickly pulled out the sandwich fixings and made herself one and two for him. She really didn't mind feeding him; lunch wasn't included, dinner was. Yet Jenner had booked in advance and would be here maybe as long as a week. So, as long as she offered, and he accepted, it just made sense to feed him. "*A happy guest,*" she muttered to herself.

"Did you say something?" he asked, from behind her.

She spun around and stared. "How can you be so quiet when you're not even on two legs?"

"I am on two legs," he corrected her, with a happy grin. "Just one of them is not made of flesh and blood."

She nodded. "The fact that you can even walk as silently as you do just blows me away."

"I spent a lot of years learning how to move quietly through the bush." He laughed. "It's not necessarily the easiest thing now that I have one prosthetic and one leg, but it's not the hardest."

"I'll take your word for it." She handed him a plate with the two sandwiches and said, "Come sit with me."

He looked down at his plate with two double-decker sandwiches. "Wow."

She shrugged. "I saw how much you ate last night. I'm not sure if you're still healing from all your injuries or if you're just one of those guys who eats large," she noted, "but I'll never let anybody in my life starve."

"You are good people."

"I try to be," she replied cheerfully. "I went through a bad patch, where I was the butt of a lot of jokes for a long time. It makes me very aware of how cruel the world can be."

He looked over at her and raised his eyebrows. "I'd love to hear more, but I can guess that it's personal. So I understand if you don't want to share."

She nodded. "Very personal *but*, when Laura comes around, she's just as likely to mention something. So it might be easier—especially if you'll be around for a few days and getting to know the locals—if you do know." She stopped, then frowned. "Or not."

"You do what you need to do. I'm not here to judge."

"Well, that would be nice for a change," she muttered, as she looked at him and sighed. "I got pregnant at the end of high school and was the butt of all the jokes for that. I kept the baby, which ended up causing me some more trouble, as my son was born with a hole in his heart. He went through multiple surgeries to try to fix the issue and ended up not …" Her voice halted at the painful reminders. "He passed away at three months."

He stared at her, and she swallowed hard. Then she realized he had reached across the table and was actually holding her hand. She looked down at her fingers entwined with his. "I didn't even see when you did that."

"And I didn't mean to, in any way, bring up something so painful," he said, his voice solemn.

"Yet sometimes it's good to talk about those who have gone before us. It helps to keep the memory alive." She brushed back the tear in her eye and pointed at his remaining sandwich.

"Now that we've dealt with it, you can eat." She picked

up her sandwich and took a bite, deliberately taking a little bit larger bite than necessary, so she had to chew and focus on that.

"Sometimes the hardest things in life," he murmured, as he ate, "are the things that mean the most."

Startled, she stared at him and then asked, "Are you talking about your accident or my son?"

"Both, because your life was enriched by having him, but that didn't make the journey any easier."

"No, it definitely didn't," she agreed.

"And why would Laura mention any of it?"

"Every once in a while she brings up comments like that. … *Remember what it was like when you were pregnant in high school?* or *Good thing you don't still have a baby to support.*"

"That's very insensitive of her," he replied in shock.

She looked at him sideways. "Yeah, like you don't really know what she's like?"

He just continued to stare.

"Are you serious? You don't know what she's like?"

"No," he stated. "I don't think the woman I knew would have ever said that."

"She certainly went through some changes these last few years, as she became more of a person of means in this town," Kellie explained.

"And yet you're friends."

"We're more *acquaintances*. Not sure I would ever be welcomed over at her house."

At that, he shook his head, frowning. "Obviously she's changed because the person I knew," he murmured, "would have never stood on ceremony, and she never would have made a friend not feel welcome."

"How long ago was this?"

He shrugged. "We got married about ten years ago, and she basically walked out of my life about … eight years ago."

"Wow, the marriage wasn't very long."

"No, it was kind of a whirlwind romance. We spent a lot of time together back then. We thought we knew exactly what we wanted, dug into marriage—because I had to leave for an overseas navy tour—and thought we were doing okay, thought we would be one of the lucky ones, and we could do this. I thought we could pass through all these hardships and become something much stronger, and then, out of the blue, I found out—while I was overseas—that she was filing for divorce." He stared down at the sandwich in his hand and swallowed hard.

"I'm sorry," Kellie said. "I didn't mean to bring up painful memories on your side."

He looked at her, then shook his head and snorted. "You know what? I don't think I've ever told anybody about that."

"It seems to be our day for sharing secrets with strangers."

"Hey, now that you know my secrets," he stated, "you can't be a stranger."

She chuckled. "I think that's a ditto for me too, although I'm not sure what it is about you that makes you so easy to talk to."

"And I guess that goes both ways as well," he confirmed. "I really hadn't seen that kind of behavior out of Laura before."

"So tell me honestly"—she looked at Jenner sideways—"are you still carrying a torch for her?"

At that, he put down his sandwich, twisted ever-so-slightly so he could face Kellie, and replied, "The woman walked out of my life without any warning, telling me that she was marrying my best friend, and sent me the divorce paperwork overseas. She didn't think that I even deserved a personal phone call. I tried hard to call her when I was over there to find out what the hell was going on, and basically she refused to accept my phone calls. Then I heard later how she was still single, so I wasn't sure what was going on. A friend of mine suggested, while I was here, that I clear the air, so I could at least move on myself."

"And that's all you're trying to do with Laura?" she asked.

"Yes," he replied. "I don't think I knew her very well, given some of the stories you're telling me, or she's changed too much for me to even recognize her now."

"She's changed," Kellie noted instantly. "Or maybe she was always like this, and you just didn't know the real Laura. When I knew her in high school, she was older than me and ..." Kellie stopped. "It really feels like we're talking about her, doesn't it?"

"That's because we are," he stated. "And maybe we shouldn't be, but it would certainly help me to understand what's going on with her before I meet her."

"You really think you'll meet up with her?"

"I asked to meet with her. Whether she does or not, I don't know."

"Interesting that you'd still want to," she remarked, staring at her sandwich on her plate, her gut twisting.

"And yet why not?" he asked. "Particularly if it's something that various people seem to think that I should."

"Sometimes I wonder if all these *various people* are actually on our side or not."

He burst out laughing at that. "Oh my, I hear you there.

I had to see all kinds of therapists after my accident. Sometimes I wondered whose side they were on. Some of the things that they wanted me to do made me swear pretty heavily."

"I'm sure." She chuckled. "I went to counseling after ... to grief counseling, you know?" she added.

"And did it help?"

"I think it did," she murmured. "It didn't help knowing that my friends and family had turned their backs on me. My parents were there, while Quincy was alive and struggling to live, but my parents hadn't been supportive through my entire pregnancy. However, I do think Quincy's life and death helped my parents to get over my mother's infidelity. Quincy's death devastated me though," she muttered. "I felt even more deserted and bereft than I had before."

"I'm sure parents aren't supposed to bury their children. Parents are supposed to die first."

"No, we should never go through that." She gave him an odd smile. "So now that we've got all that personal stuff out of the way, what's your plan for the afternoon?"

"I'll go see Jim at the hospital. I did check in this morning, and he had surgery yesterday on his leg. I can go talk to him"—he checked his watch—"after one."

"I think that's pretty standard here," she noted.

"And you've never met him?"

"Sure, as a kid, but I haven't seen him in years. The last time was, maybe a few years back. I didn't recognize this squatter guy as not being Jim. Honestly, the squatter didn't look like he was Jim, but he didn't *not* look like Jim. And ... I guess that just sounds stupid."

"Not at all, especially if you've been through a lot yourself."

"Well, Jim has been too," she noted. "I know he went into the service. His parents weren't very happy about it, but, at the same time, I think they were also proud that he was doing something for his country."

"Of course. You get mixed reactions with family all the time. Basically they just hope that you come home alive and well. I imagine that'll always be their first and foremost thought."

She got up, collected his plate, and just then the doorbell rang.

He looked at her and asked, "Are you expecting anyone?"

She shook her head. "No, but it's a bed-and-breakfast, so, hey, I get a lot of calls, door knocks all the time." She reached for his empty plate. "Are you done?"

"I'm done." He stood, as she left to put his plate in the sink. "I don't need anything else."

He walked with her to the front door. She hated to say it, but it was nice to have somebody here, almost as if he were keeping an eye on her. Of course he wasn't; there was no need for him to, but she opened the door to find the sheriff standing there.

He tilted his hat at her. "Kellie, I need to ask you a few questions."

"Right." She'd have to deal with this now, having successfully put this whole mess out of her mind for the last little while. She turned and watched as Jenner greeted the sheriff.

Jenner put a hand on her shoulder. "I'll head out to the hospital now. You're fine here?"

She nodded immediately. "I'm fine. Say hi to Jim for me."

"Will do." Jenner nodded at the sheriff and walked out.

AN ODD STRAIN filled the air as Jenner walked outside. He cast another look back at the sheriff, who stood awkwardly at the doorway. She hadn't invited him in. It being a bed-and-breakfast, he could have just walked right in anyway, without bothering to ring the bell. The front door was propped open, but the sheriff stood there on the porch, as if knowing he wouldn't be welcomed inside.

Had he had anything to do with the group who had hurt Kellie or her son, Quincy? Sometimes people cringed at the littlest shit people did. Kellie was a nice lady, and, if her story were true, and she'd gotten pregnant in high school, where the hell was the father? Jenner should have asked her.

He never understood why it was always the moms who got into trouble. It took two to tango, and, at that age, well, it was pretty damn easy to make those kinds of mistakes.

But those questions were at the back of Jenner's mind. And her conversations about Laura didn't seem to fit either. But then he hadn't seen his ex-wife in a very long time. She'd always wanted to be *somebody*. Obviously she'd found a way to become somebody's somebody. And, for her, that was probably as much ladder climbing that she could do. Never had she worked 9-to-5, and yet she always expected Jenner to come home and to look after her. Not to keep getting deployed. Of course he did. It was his job with the navy. She knew that before she married him. Still, she had walked out on him.

She'd had aspirations of him going into politics at one point in time. As he thought about it, he realized that she really hadn't known who Jenner was. If ever he did not belong somewhere, it was in politics.

He might handle something like being a sheriff because he could kick butt, even with only one leg, but politics? No way. As far as he was concerned, most politicians were just slimy.

But he knew thinking about Laura was a dangerous pathway to go down because he didn't really want anything about Laura to affect him going forward. He still held anger inside him for what she'd done. He certainly hadn't been the only serviceman out there who had taken a hard hit from a wife, who was tired of waiting for her military husband to come home.

When he went through his divorce, a couple other guys in his unit had gone through something similar. It created an ugly sentiment against women at the time.

Now seated in his rental vehicle, Jenner took another look at the sheriff and his body language, noting it was stiff, almost beseeching in a way. Jenner wasn't sure if that described the situation correctly, but it was like the sheriff knew he wasn't welcome here, and he was sorry about it. There was no arrogance; there was no aggressiveness to his stance.

Frowning, Jenner wondered if she'd be open to explaining that relationship when Jenner returned. But first he had to go see Jim.

At the hospital, he walked up the stairs to the proper room and knocked on the open door. When someone called out from inside the room, Jenner poked his head around the door and asked, "Hey, are you up for a visitor?"

Jim stared at him for a long moment. "I vaguely remember you," he admitted, "but I really don't remember ... from where."

Jenner stepped forward, reached out a hand to shake Jim's and said, "I'm the guy who found you."

Jim's face lit up in a big smile. "Wow, I know I was in rough shape out there, but I didn't realize I wouldn't even recognize you."

"I don't expect you to recognize anything. Shock can be like that."

"Well, that's pretty close to what happened," he confirmed. "Now if only I can find the asshole who put me down."

"I'm sorry. It looks, from the footprints on the surrounding ground, that you gave him a good fight."

"Well, I tried. Nothing like taking a guy by surprise, not giving me a good chance to fight back."

"Bullies are always the worse assholes, aren't they? They don't care and will take advantage of any weakness."

At that, Jim nodded.

"I checked out your house, "Jenner added. "I don't know if you checked your phone, but I emailed you the photos of the place."

"I saw that," he murmured. "Thanks for that much. I can't believe this guy cleaned out my parents' home."

"If it was just furniture," Jenner suggested, "it's all replaceable."

"And it is, but you know there were also some family mementos and bills and mail and legal documents and such."

"Well, if any of that were in the kitchen, you're good to go." Jenner laughed. "There's even food still in the fridge."

Jim stared at him.

"I returned this morning, taking another look for any sign of the War Dog or of this asshole squatter living there, but I only found a bit of food and dishes and cooking stuff and the like."

"Why would he take everything else and leave that?" he asked curiously.

"I figured it wasn't worth carting off and selling, or, wherever he was going, he already had it, or maybe you surprised him, and he had to leave earlier than expected."

"All of those kind of make sense," Jim muttered.

"Yeah, in a big way. What did the doctor have to say about your leg?"

"Surgery yesterday, haven't heard from the doctor yet today," Jim replied. "I'm going nowhere quickly, that's for sure."

"Been there, done that," Jenner noted comfortably. He looked down at the prosthetic propped up against the wall nearby. "I guess you don't need to wear that while you're in bed."

"No, I sure don't," he agreed. "I need to get a new one anyway."

"Why's that?"

"It keeps soring up the leg. You can only do so much with these damn things."

"I do know somebody who's really good at building them," Jenner stated. "If you want me to hook you up afterward, we can see about getting you something much better to walk with."

Jim looked over at Jenner and said, "Actually somebody is out in New Mexico who I really want to deal with, but, you know, she's so damn backed up."

"You're talking about Kat." Jenner lifted his foot on the edge of the hospital bed and pulled up his pant leg. "This is one of her old models that she made a couple tweaks to, so

I'm putting it to the test, before we build the new one."

Jim stared at Jenner. "You know her?" Excitement started to break through his voice.

"Absolutely," Jenner confirmed. "I've worked with her for a couple years now. She is brilliant. I mean, like I'm serious. She's quite brilliant. They actually sent me here on this job."

"Man, I'd absolutely love to get something from her that actually works."

"An awful lot of prosthetic makers are out there who build stuff that works these days, but Kat's designs are at a whole different level. Her prosthetics are like none other."

"And you're so lucky to have one of hers," Jim stated enviously. "Man, you are so damn lucky."

"Well, get yourself healed and off that bed and back home again, and I'll introduce you. I can almost pretty well guarantee you that she can do something to make your life a little bit more comfortable."

"Yeah, she's also expensive as hell," he muttered.

"We'll see. I can't promise any help along that line, but I know that she's damn good. She also does payment plans, so I know she'll work something out."

"Maybe," he stated. "Already I have to get my house together, and now some asshole's gone and stolen everything, so I don't even have a chair to sit on."

"Good thing you'll be here for a while, isn't it?"

He stared at Jenner. "I really do appreciate all you've done." And real sincerity was in his voice.

"Like I said, I've been there, done that," he said. "Absolutely nothing like this stage of life that you're going through right now. People don't understand, unless they've already been there."

Jim nodded glumly. "Isn't that the truth. Losing my leg the way I did, I wasn't coming home anytime soon and then, after my folks were killed, it just made it even harder in some ways."

"We all process grief differently," Jenner stated. "Don't judge yourself for doing it the way you need to."

"Yeah, you mean in a bottle?" he muttered.

"If it's a bottle, and it helped you and hurt no one else, then good. Now ditch the bottle and get back on your feet. I'm sure some secondhand furniture is something that we can easily find for cheap. You've already got a kitchen full of cooking stuff there and food, some of which probably needs to be tossed, but some of it will keep, and the rest of what you'll need, well, it'll take a bit of a time. But, if you own the house, that's actually a huge bonus."

"It is huge," he agreed. "I guess I was prepping myself for the day I came home to deal with it all, and instead it feels like now I'm dealing with a completely different issue." He stopped and added, "It feels like my parents' memories have been violated."

"Ah, you know that makes a lot of sense. I'm sorry about that. It's not as if we don't have enough shit to deal with in our world without having to fend off creeps who make our lives even more miserable."

At that, Jim looked at Jenner's leg and asked, "How did you lose your leg?"

"On a mission in Iraq," he replied. "I did two tours, and the second tour is when I came home kind of messed up."

"Got it. I was Air Force myself."

"Good for you. The military always needs good men. It sucks that we're both in the same boat, both injured. But, hey, at least I know what you're going through, and you know that I do understand. So, anytime you need a hand, you give me a shout."

"What are you even doing in town?" Jim asked curiously. At that, Jenner filled him in on the War Dog. "You know what? I remember you saying something about that. That was a good dog. My parents loved him."

"But the sheriff said that he came by and did a wellness check, after your mom and dad passed away, just to make sure no animals were still in need, and the sheriff never saw any sign of the War Dog."

"Well, that sheriff is a bit of a dick anyway, so I'm not sure that he would have done a whole lot, even if he had shown up to supposedly look after the dog. Probably left the door open and just let the dog run."

"Seriously?" Jenner asked, looking at Jim.

"Yeah, he's a bit of a hard-ass when it comes to dogs."

"Yet this squatter guy, who took over your house, had several running around and terrorizing Kellie. She was pretty rattled by all them," Jenner shared.

"Who's that?"

"The bed-and-breakfast owner where I'm staying."

"Ah, Kellie." Jim nodded. "Now she's a sweet girl and had a pretty rough start in life already."

"I heard a little bit about it from her," Jenner noted, with a nod.

"Well, I'm sure you heard about her son, who was the apple of her eye, even though he didn't make it very long," Jim said. "I only know from my parents. I saw her in school, but she was way younger than I was, so I didn't really get to know her. According to my parents, she's a really lovely young lady. My folks told me that the town hadn't been very generous to her."

"And why not? It's not as if anybody in town hasn't made a mistake or two."

"You kidding? That town's *perfect*," he replied, with an eye roll.

"Yeah, apparently."

"And the stupid mayor in town is rooting for a bigger political spot. He's just an egotistical asshole."

"What's his name?"

"Silas somebody or the other. He got himself one of those little arm-candy wives. My parents couldn't stand her—or him for that matter."

"That's sad too then," Jenner noted. "Sounds like your parents really knew the town well, and they would have been good for the dog."

"They loved that dog," he said instantly. "They'd be heartbroken to know anything happened to him."

"Then I'm glad that Sisco at least had that time with them." Jenner added, "I need to find that dog though, and fast."

"And what if somebody shot it?" Jim asked.

"Then I need to know for sure that Sisco was shot, and maybe I can't do anything to help him, but I sure as hell hope to find him alive and well. And maybe I can make his end of days happier than it has been so far."

"Well, you know, if I was back on my feet, I'd take him."

"And, once you're back on your feet, I'll consider it." Jenner smiled. "But you'll be recovering for a while, before looking after a dog like that is an option."

"Yeah, I will," he agreed, "but that doesn't mean it's all bad."

"No, it's not all bad. In fact, none of it's bad. You survived, and it takes a lot of guts to do that. So don't ever feel bad about losing a fight to a guy who blindsided you. That's on that asshole. It's not on you."

"And yet somehow," Jim muttered, "it feels like it's all on me."

CHAPTER 5

AFTER THE SHERIFF left, paying a visit that she felt incredibly uncomfortable with, Kellie closed her front door behind him and sat down at the reception desk. She didn't even know what to think. She'd told him exactly what had happened with the neighbor and his angry pack of dogs. The sheriff hadn't said that he disbelieved her; he hadn't said anything. Just made a comment that he wished that she'd said something to him about the dogs earlier, and he would have taken care of it.

He had stated it in such a way that she almost believed him, but Kellie had had enough problems with him and his wife that Kellie didn't trust anything he said anymore. Not a lot of the locals either. Which was kind of sad because, in her own hometown, she wanted to feel like she could be safe here. She wanted to feel like everything would be okay. Yet she'd gotten pregnant here, and, of course, the sheriff's son had been Kellie's boyfriend and Quincy's father. Whether the sheriff remembered any of that, she didn't know.

His son was a trucker, and right now he was gone a lot. She wanted to laugh at that because he'd planned to be somebody big, but, when it came down to it, he got his latest girlfriend pregnant, and they recently got married, and now he was off trucking, trying to pay the bills to support them.

At least he had married this woman, once he got her

pregnant.

He'd ditched Kellie right before the prom, and Kellie was already pregnant, just didn't know it yet. When she did figure it out, she had fully planned on raising the child on her own. The situation had been dire for her, given her parents' lack of support, yet it had only made her doubly want this child.

When her son had been born sick, it had been the most devastating thing she'd ever experienced. Her parents had quickly come on board when they heard the news, and they'd been just as devastated. It had been a roller coaster ride for three months that had ended in pain and torment for them all. The only good thing to come out of it was the fact that her parents had finally made peace with each other. Kellie and her mom still didn't talk about Quincy or why her mom cheated on her dad. Just not a whole lot to say about either that didn't bring up bad memories.

As the sheriff backed away from the B&B and disappeared down the road, almost immediately Laura's sports car pulled in. Kellie got up and went outside to meet her. Laura stepped out slowly, using the car door for support. Kellie groaned at that. "Now why are you here?" she murmured to herself. Generally Laura wasn't somebody willing to spend time anywhere close to this part of town.

When Kellie invited her inside, they both headed to the front room, where Laura asked, "You have a male guest here, right?"

She looked at her. "Yeah, I have one guest. Why?" But she already knew why.

"Please tell me that he's not six-two, really fit, and a hot-tie."

She stared at her. "He's like six-two, maybe early thirties, and, yeah, I guess you'd call him handsome." Actually he was a drop-dead hottie, but no way Kellie would say that to Laura. "Why?"

"I'm afraid he might be my ex." At that, Laura sat down in a side chair and groaned. "Why would he do this to me?"

"What do you mean?" Kellie asked in confusion. "The guest I have is here after a War Dog."

"Of course he'll be after a War Dog. What the hell's a War Dog anyway? We don't send dogs to war. What kind of stupid idiot would say that? He's such a drama queen."

Kellie's jaw dropped at that. "This guy's not a drama queen," she argued in a high-pitched voice. She kept telling herself to get it together, and this was so not the conversation that she wanted to be a part of. "Look. I'm not sure what this is all about, but what difference does it make?"

"Because Silas doesn't know much about him. We don't talk about it. At all," Laura snapped promptly, "and he'll be pissed if he finds out my ex is here."

"What'll he find out? Their lives are far apart, and their paths aren't likely to cross, are they?"

At that, Laura looked at her speculatively. "You know what? You're probably right. I mean, why would they run into each other? I am worrying for nothing."

"Why be worried at all? You've been married how long now?"

"I know. I know. *I know*, but, we didn't exactly leave on good terms."

"I'm sure you divorced and had a chance to talk everything through." Kellie shrugged. "What could possibly be *bad terms?*"

At that, Laura stared at Kellie. "You're such an innocent."

Her jaw dropped. "Seriously?" She laughed. "I'm the last person anybody in this town would call an innocent."

"Even getting knocked up like you did is so typical of an innocent," Laura noted. "Anybody else would have just had an abortion and moved on."

At that, her heart clamped in pain. "And I would have missed out on a love that remains one of the best experiences of my life," Kellie stated.

"Whatever, but still, you were too young for it."

Kellie didn't know what to say. She hadn't seen Laura in this kind of mood before. "Do you want a cup of tea?"

"No, I'm sitting here, wondering what to do about him."

"I don't even know that it is him," Kellie noted, "and he's out right now at the hospital."

"What's he doing at the hospital?" she asked in amazement.

"He's gone to see Jim, my neighbor."

"Okay, whatever," she said, already dismissing it out of hand, as if she really didn't want to know anything.

It was so odd for Kellie to see Laura like this and to actually think of Jenner being married to her. "How was your marriage to him?" she asked.

"We got divorced," she snapped, "so that should tell you everything. He was always gone, never home, never made any money. We never had any fun. And believe me. At that time of life, fun is important." she declared with such emphasis, as if to say that most people didn't understand how important fun was.

Considering that Kellie had skipped fun because she'd given birth at seventeen, there wasn't a whole lot she could say about that. "Maybe, but it sounds like probably you guys weren't suited at all."

"I was in love with the romance of it," she replied short-ly, and then she sighed. "Which sounds trite and stupid now."

"It doesn't matter. You're happily married. You're preg-nant with your first child. I'm sure it'll all be just fine."

"Maybe," Laura huffed, as she pulled herself up. "Can't wait until this baby is born though. It's like dragging around a beached whale everywhere with you."

For Kellie, she'd loved being pregnant; she'd loved hav-ing that little being inside her, that person who would love her just because of who she was, instead of hating her just because of who she was. "I'm sure the birth will happen soon enough," she offered supportively.

At that, Laura looked over at her, adding an eye roll. "Again we're back to that whole thing about how *you're way too nice for your own good.*"

"I am who I am," she stated, with a smile.

"Yeah, I hear you," she muttered. "Well, don't say any-thing to him. I don't know if it is him or not," she noted. "I'll have to meet him somewhere but not here, definitely not here."

"What's wrong with here?" Kellie asked, looking around at her huge farmhouse. "Lots of places are here where you two can talk privately."

"Oh, God no," she spat, with a shudder. "If you spent a hundred thousand to update this place, it would be much better."

"But I don't have one hundred thousand." Kellie frowned, as she realized how Laura felt about her home. "Look. You don't have to have your family stay here either."

"I wouldn't normally," she said, with a careless hand

wave. "But everybody in town is booked up, and I really don't want them spread all across town. They'll probably hate being here, but it's the best answer." And, with that, she made her way to the door. "I'll talk to you later." And she walked out.

After having some of the most insulting bombs dropped on her, Kellie didn't know what to think and just stared.

AS HE WALKED out of the hospital, Jenner checked for the addresses of the local veterinarians. There was just one in the next town over. He headed straight there. Soon as he walked in, he asked if it were possible to talk to the vet.

The woman immediately shook her head. "Lord no, not today especially. It's surgery day."

"Ah, well, maybe I can leave a message, and we can find a moment when I can speak to him, even if it's just on the phone."

"Sure." She pulled a pad of paper toward him. "What's going on?" When he explained what he was here for, her jaw dropped. "A War Dog here in town?"

He nodded. "Yes, exactly, a War Dog here in town. It's been here for several months with the Stippletones, until they died. But now the dog has been on its own for a couple months."

She winced. "They were killed in that car accident."

"So I heard."

"Nobody's seen the dog since. Apparently the sheriff went to check for any animals but didn't find any."

He watched her face intently but found no sign that she thought maybe the sheriff would have done anything either.

"I'll tell the doctor, but I can tell you right now that I haven't seen any dogs quite along that description."

"Looks like a black shepherd." He pulled up a picture of Sisco on his phone and showed it to her.

She looked at it and nodded. "Really does look like a shepherd."

"Unless you know the breed differences, it's pretty hard to tell them apart."

"Okay, good enough," she said. "I'll let him know, but I can tell you that he's tied up for most of the day."

"Got it," Jenner noted. "Are there any other vets around here?"

"Not in town but one is not too far away on the way to the next town," she noted. "So you can check in there with him too." And, with her handwritten directions, Jenner headed off to the second clinic. When he explained what was going on to the next vet, he immediately shook his head. "No, haven't seen anything like that. If I had a dog in, I would have automatically scanned him, particularly one that's got that kind of breeding or training. That would have triggered a search for the dog's owners."

"Right. So chances are this War Dog hasn't been brought in for treatment anywhere because of that added military ID chip, right?"

"That would be my guess," he noted. "There is an older lady on the other side of town, where animals often seem to find their way to. She found a couple aggressive dogs that were homeless and was afraid that somebody had shot them. When she could get close enough, one had already died from his wounds. She came in with the other dog, and it was badly injured."

"Was?"

"Yeah, we had to put him down."

"And it was shot?"

The vet nodded. "The woman was pretty devastated."

Jenner quickly explained to this vet about the neighbor with the angry pack of dogs.

At that, the vet's eyebrows shot up. "You know that sounds like one of them. The woman told me how the dog came to her, bleeding, and she looked after it. She mentioned how it wasn't fighting her, so she figured it had to be pretty badly hurt. She brought it in to me, and unfortunately there was not a whole lot I could do. Already badly infected and all."

"Okay. Any chance I can get some contact information for the woman?" When the vet hesitated, Jenner quickly added, "Or could you contact this lady and ask her if she would speak to me?"

The vet nodded. "That I can do." He stepped out of the room, and, when he returned a few minutes later, he said, "Martha would be happy to talk to you. Here's her phone number, and here's her address. Good luck."

And, with that, the vet called for the next patient and headed back into his exam rooms.

Jenner returned again to the bed-and-breakfast. Mostly his instincts were taking him there to ensure Kellie was okay. He pulled in, seeing nobody else in the parking lot. He pulled up to the front and hopped out, walked inside and called out, "Hey, I'm here."

She walked through to the front and gave him a wry smile. "Good timing on your part."

"Why's that?" he asked.

"Because the sheriff's gone and so is Laura."

"Ah, and does she know?"

"She asked me about you. Apparently the rumor mill's already going double-time."

"Yeah, what can you expect in a place like this?" he asked. Kellie quickly passed over the little bit of the conversation that she'd had with Laura earlier that concerned Jenner. "Ouch. You seem to be …" And then he hesitated.

"Yeah, I'm smarting from a couple comments that she made, so, if my tone sounds a little snippy, that's why."

"Maybe you should tell me everything," he suggested.

She shrugged. "No point," she muttered.

But it didn't take long for Jenner to get the story out of Kellie. "I'm sorry. I guess there was always that bitchy side to her."

"Not so much even a bitchy side," Kellie noted, "but I didn't know she was even looking down at my place that way. You know how it's funny that you consider you're friends, until you realize how somebody really feels toward you, and you didn't see it until then."

"Of course not and you know what? Short of that conversation where she came here to confirm I was in town, and she was obviously upset about it, you never would have seen that part of her," he suggested. "You wouldn't have known still."

She nodded slowly. "Doesn't make me feel any better."

"Of course not," he agreed. "Yet also we know that that's who she is."

Kellie's shoulders sagged, and she nodded. "And here, just hours earlier, you were the one telling me how she wasn't like that."

"No, I didn't see it back then," he noted. "And yet I do remember certain conversations with various people, including a friend of mine, who was like, *Dude, why are you even marrying her?* But I was in love, so there's that," he stated, with a smirk. *"Apparently stupid in love."*

"Well, it's a common phrase," she agreed, "and you're certainly not the only one."

He nodded. "How come there's animosity between you and the sheriff?"

She hesitated and then sighed. "His son was the father of my child."

At that, his eyebrows shot up. "Ouch, that wouldn't have made for a good time."

"No, sure wouldn't have, and, of course, no matter what I said, his son wouldn't back up my stories, so the sheriff thinks I made it all up."

"Wow. I'm sorry about that too. Sounds like both father and son are asses."

"Yep, both are," she confirmed. "The only good thing is that his son is now married to somebody else he got knocked up recently, and he's working as a trucker to support them. So he drives through town all the time. We basically ignore each other."

"Did you actually go out with him?"

She looked at him sharply. "Yeah. Remember that prom night story I told? That was him. We'd been going out for months. And he didn't even tell me that we were broken up and that he was taking my best friend to the prom."

He winced. "Hey, sorry. I didn't mean it quite the way it came out. I was asking if you'd been in a relationship for a long time."

"Yeah, well, I was seventeen. So I thought we were in a relationship for a long time, if you count a couple months as a *long time.*"

At that, he almost snickered, holding it in, until he

caught the humor in her voice and the expression on her face. "You know what? It's really good to have a sense of humor over shit like this."

"Because of shit like this," she noted, shaking her head, "sometimes I wonder why I even stay."

"So let me ask you that. Why do you stay?"

"Because of this place, the bed-and-breakfast. It was my grandparents' originally. I loved it. I grew up here, always wanting to be the one who took it over and ran it. I thought, when I had my son, it would be perfect for us, you know? … I can stay home with him, make an income, look after my family. We'd all be good."

"And then it didn't quite work out that way, *huh?*"

"No, it sure didn't." She sighed. "Anyway, just a heads-up that Laura does think that you're here, and the sheriff has a bit of history with me. So, if you're looking for help from him, I'm really not sure if he'd give it to you."

"I think he'll give it to me," Jenner stated, "but I gather you feel like he won't give you the time of day."

"No, I sure don't. I guess I can't blame him. At the time I was pretty irate about his son." She shrugged. "Obviously it was for the best."

"Well, the sheriff also lost out," Jenner noted. "That was his grandson who passed away."

"I know, and there's nothing like going through what I went through to make you grow up quickly. And, when you grow up, you learn to forgive and forget," she admitted. "So maybe I haven't quite learned to forgive everybody, but I'm working on it."

"At least you're doing better than I am," Jenner said. "It was suggested that I come here and talk to my ex, but, at the time, I was like, *Yeah, hell no.*"

She chuckled. "And here I think it's a good idea, if for no other reason that you'll upset her."

He burst out laughing. "In other words, if it upsets Laura now, you're all for it."

"That makes me sound terribly bitchy too, doesn't it?" She shook her head. "And I don't mean it that way."

"No, but you're human, and you've been hurt."

She raised both hands in frustration. "And you know what? I have homemade ice cream in the back. Would you want some?"

"Homemade?"

She glanced at him. "Yeah, I make ice cream when I get upset."

"*Sure*," he said, "but you do know that you'll never make money out of your bed-and-breakfast if you keep feeding me."

She smiled. "No, maybe not, but you're good for my soul." She led the way to the kitchen, opened up a second freezer he hadn't even seen off in the storeroom, and he whistled. "Are you serious? Is this all ice cream?"

She nodded. "It occurred to me that, maybe down the road, if I ever get there, it might be something I could set up to sell."

He stared at her. "Oh my God, let me try some. The restaurants around here would probably love it."

"Well, restaurants in town might love it," she noted, "but, around here, I think my name's mud."

"Your name's not mud," he argued. "And, if it was mud, it shouldn't still be mud."

She shrugged. "Nothing like long memories from people."

"Screw them," he said easily.

She burst out laughing. "Good point, so screw them." She studied the labels on her tubs. "What flavor do you like?"

"Choices?" he asked hesitantly.

"Oh, I've got half a dozen here," she stated, "and a couple more." She pulled out several, looked at them, and asked, "How about these?"

"I like all ice cream," he said. "Don't you?"

She grinned at that. "Now if all my guests were as amiable as you, I'd be doing just fine."

"Yeah, are you surviving here?"

"Well, yes and no," she replied. "The bed-and-breakfast really helps. I don't have a mortgage, and that also really helps, and I board some horses too. So I don't have many expenses, just me and the household bills. I do have an online presence, which I guess might sound weird, but I do a lot of cooking and baking videos, and so I have quite a few people who follow me there. I'm even starting to get endorsements."

"As long as they don't follow you back home again," he warned her, "I'm all for it."

She nodded. "Nobody knows where I live. I've given the state but not the town."

"Right, I guess that's always the hazard online, isn't it?"

"If I could just cook for a living," she noted, "I would be fine, but I don't want to go and actually"—she stopped, stared at him—"I know it sounds absolutely ridiculous, but I don't want to work nine to five."

Ice cream in hand, she went to her kitchen and put them on the counter. Next she pulled out a container with powdered mix inside, then pulled out a funky machine he'd never seen before and plugged it in. She quickly added some of the dry goods to some liquid and mixed up a batter. He watched, wanting to ask what she was doing but not sure that he should.

When she poured the batter onto the machine—something like a waffle iron—he was even more confused. "Do you want me to serve the ice cream. It is out of the freezer."

"It is, and it will be much easier to scoop up when it's not quite so hard. So ice cream is always better if you just let it sit for a moment or two."

He wanted to say something about it being longer than a moment or two, but, when the machine in front of her beeped, she quickly opened it up, and—from one side to the other—she rolled up the crispy toasted dough, and he stopped dead in wonder. "You just made cones," he stated in amazement.

She nodded and gave him a big grin. "Yeah, I did." And she poured the second portion of the batter into the machine.

"Wow." He stared at the cone now sitting, cooling on a plate. "You know that a lot of people would not go to that kind of effort."

"But I like cooking," Kellie said, "and this, for me, is a special effort as much as it's fun. I think I've got this recipe perfected," she said, tapping the container.

"So you just take some of that premade mix and add a liquid?"

She nodded. "And the trick is, you have to roll the waffle as soon as it comes out, then let it cool. If it has a chance to cool before you shape it, then it snaps." When the second cone was done, she unplugged the machine, put away her mix, and brought the two cones over to the table, where the ice cream sat.

She opened the tubs, and, with the cooler of the two cones, she scooped in one scoop of each of the three kinds. Then she handed him the cone. He stared at the concoction in front of him. She asked, "Is something wrong?"

And such worry was in her voice that he shook his head. "No, nothing is wrong at all," he said. "I don't think I've ever had homemade ice cream in a homemade cone."

"Well, hopefully you'll like it," she noted. "If not, ... you don't have to eat it. Just throw it in the garbage."

He shook his head in amazement. "No, that's not happening," he muttered. He took a tentative sample of his ice cream, while she served up hers. And then closed his eyes and took a second sample.

She quickly put away the ice cream tubs, and, when she returned, she asked, "What's wrong?"

"Wrong? Nothing," he said, opening his eyes. "I'm savoring."

She beamed. "See? That's how people should enjoy food. I mean, it's meant to be enjoyed. I don't get why it ends up being something that you just cook haphazardly so you can eat fast."

"Because, for most of us, that's all we can handle doing in the kitchen," he noted in a dry tone.

"Oh, not me," she said. "I love food. And, when my son was sick, it's what I did when I was at home, worrying. I spent as much time as I could with him in the hospital, but, when we lost the battle, cooking was my salvation," she muttered. "And, since then, it's what I do all the time."

"Oh, please don't ever stop," Jenner said, as he sat down at the kitchen table and just worked his way through the ice cream.

She burst out laughing. "If you could see your face right now," she teased.

"I know what it would look like," he stated immediately, "because this is absolutely to die for."

"Thank you." She nodded. "I am happy with these flavors." She opened the back door and added, "Want to come outside and sit?" And they sat outside in the backyard, eating the ice cream, just enjoying the pleasant company and the momentary meeting of minds.

When he looked up, he thought he saw something flash in the hills behind her.

"Who owns that land?" he asked.

"I do."

He looked at her, frowning.

She shrugged. "A fair bit of land is here, all of which my family owns. Well, technically it's mine now."

"And you actually own it all yourself?"

She nodded.

"Have you seen any animals out there?" he asked, his gaze on the horizon.

"Not really, why?"

"Just wondering. I thought I saw a dog."

"I thought I saw something dark the other night, but I wouldn't have known it was a dog. And after seeing the neighbor's dogs, I sure as hell wouldn't have thought anything good about it."

"Right." Jenner looked down at the cone that he was busy eating and said, "As soon as I'm done with this, I'll head up there and take a look."

"Why?" she asked.

"Because when I said I think I see a dog, I mean, I think I saw *my* War Dog." And, with that, he got up and quickly walked away, leaving her to stare after him.

CHAPTER 6

KELLIE DIDN'T SEE Jenner for the next hour. She worried about him out there, thinking of him getting around on his prosthetic out there on the rough terrain, then shrugged it off. If he didn't seem to care, then she certainly shouldn't. He seemed quite capable enough. When her phone rang not long afterward, she answered it to learn that he was still out there.

"Hey," he greeted her. "Do you have any dog food at home?"

"No, not at all," she said. "Why? Do you really think he's out there?"

"Well, something's out here. I'm just not sure because I think I see him, but he won't come close to me. When I get closer, he takes off."

"What else would you expect?" she asked jokingly. "It's not like you're a friend to him."

"I know. That's why I was wondering if you have any dog food," he replied. "When I get back, I'll run into town and get some." He hung up, and she hesitated at that because, well, she might not have any traditional dog food, but that didn't mean she couldn't scrounge up some food here that a dog would eat.

When he popped in a little bit later, she added, "I don't have *dog food*, dog food, but I have meat and bones."

"No, I don't want to do that," he explained. "I don't know what he's been eating, so I'll roust up something at the pet store in the center of town. They surely have something."

"Oh, they'll have something, for sure."

He raced out to his vehicle and took off.

She stared out in the hills behind her, but all she could think about was those damn wild dogs and how they had surrounded her. She'd never been frightened of dogs before, until then. She also wasn't sure if there weren't more running loose in the wings. Knowing that she had been that close to getting killed by them and ripped to pieces still woke her up in the middle of the night in a cold sweat.

It wasn't fair; she hadn't done anything to the dogs, but, of course, she didn't even know that they saw her as a threat as much as they just saw her as somebody in their way. Maybe they were just out having fun. She could imagine what any other animal must have felt like, being caught up in their clutches.

And it was scary, like seriously scary. Still, not much to be done about it now. She worked on dinner, and soon Jenner was back.

He told her, "I'll wait until it gets a little darker outside. Then I'll go look for Sisco."

"But is it safe?" she asked. "Think about it. I mean, that dog's been on its own for a long time."

"I don't know what's going on," he admitted. "I need to go out there and figure it out." He looked at her and smiled. "He won't come back after you."

"You say that," she stated, with a wry look, "but I'm not sure I believe you."

He nodded. "I get that too. I don't think that Sisco would ever be the kind that would have hurt you."

"No, but those other dogs …"

"I know." Jenner nodded. "Those other dogs are enough to scare the crap out of anybody, but two are dead."

She shrugged. "But there's two more."

At that, he nodded again. "We'll see what comes of them, but I have to get out there and see if I can track down Sisco before he gets shot."

"Dinner first," she stated firmly. "Dinner first, then you can go out."

He looked at her and asked, "What makes you think I even have any appetite for dinner? I just ate three scoops of some wonderful ice cream."

Her eyebrows shot up. "Roast chicken and all the fixings?"

"You're right," he agreed. "Dinner first."

She chuckled and said, "You can set the table, if you want to help."

"I'm okay with that." He headed to the sideboard immediately. "And thank you," he said. "Best recommendation ever to come stay with you." She looked at him in surprise, and he nodded. "I'm serious. You're a very gifted chef."

"Well, I'd like to think that I'm a good cook." She laughed. "The *gifted chef* part seems a bit much."

"Nope, not at all," he argued. "That ice cream was divine, and the cone was absolutely out of this world. You can easily sell that stuff, but, with all your time involved, I fear there won't be a whole lot of money in it for you."

"I know," she muttered, "but I was wondering about doing some of that teaching stuff online and showing other people how to do it."

"You know something? That could be a huge money-maker."

"I don't know about moneymaking," she admitted, "but I would sure like to find some joy in life again."

AN HOUR LATER, after a delicious meal, Jenner raced out to the back of the property, again catching sight of something black and dark out there. From his right-hand side, he thought he heard some barking, but the flash of black had come from the opposite side. Trusting his instincts, he headed toward the barking, and, as soon as he came close, he heard a rustling in the underbrush; it sounded like the wild dogs taking off through the area.

He wondered what the hell was going on that so many dogs were loose out here. But then, considering two had been killed, of the possible four that the squatter had, maybe the squatter had ducked out to avoid paying any fines for his dogs. Maybe the squatter had thought they were just enough of a headache and a hit to his wallet to not be bothered with rounding them up. A lot of people got animals, and then, when they required training or medical expenses, they ditched them.

Anybody who would squat in somebody else's house and who then stole its contents, after beating up the legal homeowner, leaving him injured in the ditch to die, obviously didn't give a crap about anything or anyone else in life.

Jenner moved swiftly, looking for the barking dogs. In the distance he saw two dogs, racing flat-out—one large, one smaller. A series of yells came from the direction the dogs had left. People were already on the scene of whatever was going on. Chances were the dogs had gotten into something that they shouldn't—like chickens. Jenner headed after them, but they already had a hell of a good start.

When he slowed down, he found a large pasture up ahead. He looked around but saw no sign of people or of the two dogs. As he slowly turned to look in the opposite direction, he caught sight of something dashing through his peripheral vision. Not sure if it was one of the wild dogs—or the War Dog that he was looking for—he stopped and stilled.

Letting his eyes adjust, he waited to see what might show up. Almost immediately he saw a decent-size dark-looking shape. And instinctively he knew it was the War Dog that he was looking for. His heart leapt for joy. Finally something positive. He called out "Sisco, stay," in a soft voice and then in a stronger voice repeated the command again and again and again.

When no response came, he turned to look and realized that the dog was gone. He wasn't sure what to make of that attitude because, if somebody had misused Sisco's training commands, the War Dog would experience a lot of distress. A lot of people didn't realize that there was a bond between trainer and dog as much as an obedience to the commands.

The dog had to trust the person giving the commands in order to listen, and, if Sisco had been beaten or abused, or if somebody had read some of these instructions or orders online and had used the commands to confuse or to abuse the dog for whatever reason, that kind of trust could be forever broken. But Jenner had faith in the War Dog's training and faith in the animal world, much more so than he did with people.

Swearing, he took off after Sisco, knowing there's no way he'd be fast enough. When the dog swiftly took a sharp veer to the left, Jenner followed and heard a horrific growl coming from behind him. Some other dogs—possibly the ones he'd been chasing earlier—had backtracked around behind him. He turned to see two dogs coming silently through the bush up on him, and he swore.

"Well, if you guys were the ones that surrounded Kellie and scared the crap out of her," he murmured, "no wonder she's terrified of dogs."

Although she did her best to make it look like she was okay, it was obvious that she was really unnerved at the idea of dogs now. As Jenner studied the two in front of him, both looked to be mutts, broad in the shoulder, huge heads, so some Rottie mix in there somewhere.

They stared at Jenner with a look in their eyes that said they were hungry.

"You guys haven't been fed at all, have you?" he muttered. "That's bad news because now you're hunting." Once they hunted in packs, it was even worse news for everybody around them. Only two were before him now, but that just coincided with the information that he'd already received about how they had originally been a pack of four.

He couldn't even imagine what Kellie had gone through. Thank God the dogs' owner had called them off. But then why had the squatter disappeared? Unless he'd been afraid that he would get caught—either through the antics of his killing dogs or especially once Jim showed up.

The beating Jim had taken, under any other circumstances, wouldn't have brought Jim down so easily. But, already weak from surgeries and still struggling with his own handicap, he'd been taken by surprise, and it had been a short fight after that. But it would never be okay in Jenner's books to take down a man who was already in some way healing. This squatter guy was just a shitty asshole. But

Jenner already knew that, and assholes came in all shapes and colors, so it didn't matter who and what. Jenner and Jim just had to deal with the fact that they needed to find the asshole, hopefully fast, but it wouldn't stop these dogs right now.

Jenner called out in a calm voice, "Hey, guys." One's ear twitched. "Yeah, you're not sure what happened to your world, are you?" The dog in the front stepped a paw closer and hunkered down lower.

"Yeah, I see you. And having successfully taken down God-only-knows how many animals in the last little while," he noted, "you've got a thirst for blood right now too, don't you?"

Jenner didn't have a weapon on him, and that was something he should take care of. Fighting off one dog was definitely possible. Fighting off two? Not so much. But thankfully it was only two and not the four. He hated to see good or redeemable animals get put down, but he suspected that it would end that way for these two.

He studied the second dog, as he continued to talk to them both in a calm voice. Backing up against the trunk of the closest tree, he realized that second dog was more of a follower and probably didn't have the same hunting instincts that the bigger one did. Because that bigger one, the leader, the aggressive one, looked like he would need a bullet, and it took a lot for Jenner to say that. Once they got the taste for human blood, it was pretty damn hard to stop them from killing more.

They needed fences and secured yards to be rehabilitated. Yet, when they were already this far gone, very few people could take on animals like these and succeed. And Jenner didn't blame the animals one bit; they'd been deserted by whoever it was who had had them. Jenner couldn't even be sure that the squatter guy who walked away from them had actually had them for very long. For all Jenner knew, these dogs may have been taken from the Stippletones' house that the squatter decided to live in. But, with no answers, Jenner knew that he needed calm actions right now.

At least calm until the first dog took another step forward and showed lots of teeth, followed by a low growl.

Swearing gently, Jenner reached for a branch above him, and, just as the dog surged for him, Jenner kicked up and swung onto the bottom branch. After that, it was a quick several hops to get up even higher. From that new vantage point, Jenner stared down at the pissed attack dog, as he barked at Jenner from below.

"You really would kill me, wouldn't you?" he asked, studying him. "I'm sorry about that, you know? That just won't happen today." He reached for his phone, and first thing he did was call Kellie at the bed-and-breakfast.

"Don't go outside," he snapped. "Two dogs chased me up a tree. I don't have any weapons right now, but I'll call the sheriff and get some assistance. This one dog in particular looks like he's just out for blood."

"Yeah, the one with that massive black head, isn't it?" she asked. "I remember him."

And he heard the shiver in her voice. "That's all right. We'll take care of him," he stated.

"You're in a tree," she noted, with a nervous laugh. "How do you expect anybody to take care of him?"

"Well, that'll be the trick," he admitted. "Although I think the sheriff would be all too happy to kill these two." And just then one of the dogs tried to make a jump for him. Jenner swore, as he pulled his foot up and away. "Damn tree isn't quite big enough either," he stated in a cheerful voice.

Just then, out of nowhere, came a black streak, and it plowed into the shoulder of the second dog, with one solid *thud*. The first dog spun at the noise, jumped in, snapping and snarling, and attacked the new arrival.

CHAPTER 7

KELLIE HAD TO admit to waiting on pins and needles, constantly stepping out the back door to check up at the hills and then racing to the front yard at the sound of any movement. Surely Jenner would be back soon. Just the thought of him being alone and up that tree set her nerves on edge and her tears just out of sight.

When she heard a vehicle, she raced to the front door, threw it open, a big smile on her face, only to see Laura step out. Her smile immediately dropped away. "Hey, I'm surprised to see you."

"I don't know why," she replied crossly. "Until this baby comes, all I can do is keep busy."

"I'm sure a lot of soon-to-be moms say things like that," Kellie noted, with a commiserating look.

Laura rolled her eyes. "Whatever. I should have had a surrogate."

"Oh, wow. I never thought that would be something you would want."

"Why not?" she muttered. "You look like you were expecting somebody else."

Kellie felt a flush rise on her cheeks. "No, not necessarily. I had the cops—the sheriff—come and talk to me this morning. I was expecting him back."

At that, Laura leveled Kellie with a hard stare. "Since

when do you care about the sheriff like that?"

She rolled her eyes. "Come on in. Have a seat and get comfy."

"I'm not staying. Just wanted to tell you to cancel those reservations for the family. They don't want to stay here," she stated, with an eye roll. "I convinced my husband, and he wants them to stay at our place."

"Okay." Kellie's heart sank at the thought of losing that many reservations. "I understand." She gave Laura a negligent shrug. "It is life."

"It is, indeed," she muttered. At that she heaved herself back inside her vehicle. "I'm leaving, don't want to see him."

"Or you could just talk to him and get it over with," Kellie suggested. "He seems quite nice." At that, she got a flat stare.

"Of course he does. That's the thing about him. He was always nice. He was always one of the good guys—but good guys end up last."

"I didn't realize you were so anxious to get someplace else with him."

"For the first year, I guess I thought he'd get there on his own, but it didn't seem like anything would change. I just couldn't hang around and wait for him."

"Got it," Kellie noted. "With the baby, your life will definitely change now."

She nodded. "I'm just not sure if it'll change for the better or not."

And that comment had Kellie's jaw dropping. "Seriously?"

Laura shrugged. "The only reason I'm having this baby at all is for my husband," she snapped. "Otherwise you can bet I wouldn't be going through this."

"But it is such a beautiful experience," Kellie argued, when she could speak again.

"Yeah? And what happens if it's something like what you went through?" she asked. "I'm not cut out for that kind of stuff. Not even sure at this point that there's anything maternal about me."

"Well, you won't know until you get there," Kellie replied impulsively.

"Yeah, great," Laura muttered. "Still not thrilled at the idea."

Kellie watched as Laura drove away, her heavily pregnant belly still not impeding her ability to drive. Shaking her head, Kellie considered how she had generously thought of Laura as a friend, then as an acquaintance, and now as just some rude person she saw during the school year, but, as an adult, Laura was an even ruder client, who Kellie must endure for years to come.

Kellie couldn't quite believe the things that Laura had said. Kellie was finding out more about Laura, and she wasn't exactly who Kellie had thought Laura was. Then again pregnancy sometimes also brought out the worst in everybody. Laura saw it as quite a challenge, especially what was happening to her body, particularly since Laura didn't want to be pregnant for her own sake.

When Kellie had first found out she was pregnant—at seventeen no less—she had been more shocked than overjoyed, but it certainly hadn't taken long for her to realize how special that child growing within her was. Yet she also understood that it wasn't the same for everybody. If one thing had helped Kellie, it would have been the therapy after Quincy's death and belonging to several grief support groups, where she understood—slowly, over time—that pregnancy was a different experience for everybody.

Marriage too was a different experience for everybody. Relationships, life, the reactions of the people around us, it was forever unique to all. Everyone had their own perspective, and living through those experiences changes you, and seeing Laura right now just added to it. And still it completely amazed Kellie that Laura wouldn't want that very special being she and her husband had created and was now growing in Laura's belly. It's a part of them; it's part of who they are. Kellie wondered if that meant that Laura didn't want part of herself or part of her husband either. With that contemplative thought, she headed back inside to wait, once again, for Jenner.

Kellie then laughed abruptly at whatever silly look must have been on her face when she thought Jenner was home but had faced Laura instead. *Why wasn't I honest with Laura? Why didn't I tell Laura that I was waiting for Jenner?*

JENNER HAD SPENT the last hour in the tree, wishing he could get down. Finally the wild dogs took off, and he scrambled down. As soon as he hit the ground, he heard a growl from a distance. The sheriff was on his way, so Jenner knew that that would end up badly for whichever dog remained in the area. Jenner wanted to tell him to take off, but he wasn't sure which one it was. In the distance he heard a shout. Jenner cupped his hands around his mouth and called back.

The sheriff showed up a few minutes later, and he was hot and sweaty and in quite a pissy mood. "What the hell?" he asked, shaking his head. "Those damn dogs."

"Two of the dogs tried to attack me," Jenner explained. "The third one saved me."

At that, the sheriff looked at him in disbelief. "Oh, don't tell me the one that you want to save is the one that you're trying to vouch for right now."

"Absolutely I am," Jenner snapped. "Sisco came up, hit the beta dog hard on the shoulder, and then the alpha dog went off in this massive chase of Sisco. I heard a bunch of howling in the distance, but I'm not sure who got the better part of that fight."

"Well, it would be nice if they kill each other off," the sheriff stated, his hand on his gun already. "I tell you, at this point, any dog that's not accompanied is getting a bullet." He turned to look at his deputy. The deputy nodded. The sheriff continued. "We can't have them attacking honest citizens," he noted in a hard voice.

"I certainly agree with that," Jenner admitted, "but, in this case, I'd appreciate it if you would avoid pulling a trigger on the shepherd."

"Shepherds are dangerous." The sheriff spit out what looked like chewing tobacco onto the ground.

"No, they're only dangerous in the wrong hands," Jenner countered.

"Will you take responsibility if the War Dog jumps somebody and hurts him?" the sheriff asked. "Because you know that'll lead to a lawsuit or two."

"Absolutely it could," he agreed, "and, if the dog is in my control and under my custody at that point in time, absolutely I will take responsibility for Sisco."

At that, the sheriff stared at Jenner.

Jenner nodded. "I know these dogs. I know what they're like. Now the other two? Those wild dogs? Honestly, they look like they had bloodlust in their hearts. They are the ones I'm pretty sure that surrounded Kellie."

At that, the sheriff frowned. "I sure wish she had told me about that."

"Yeah, sure wish she felt comfortable enough to," Jenner added. At that remark, he got a hard glance from the sheriff, and his deputy barely held his grin. Obviously everybody knew about the relationship issues between the sheriff and Kellie. "So thanks for coming out to my rescue," Jenner added. He deliberately avoided mentioning any of the growls that he still heard from the far end of the woods.

"We'll work around the area and see if we can come up with any sign of the dogs," the sheriff declared. "I'd much rather pop them right now and save us the trouble of hunting them down later."

"You can try," Jenner noted, "but those two looked pretty wild. Any luck on finding the guy squatting in Jim's house?"

"No, not a clue. As much as Kellie saw him, she didn't really get enough of a glance at who he was in order to be able to identify him."

"Yeah, she was too focused on her survival and the wild dogs at that time." He frowned at a further thought. "Did she tell you that he came to the B&B and banged on the door after-hours, wanting inside?"

The sheriff stared at Jenner in shock. "Hell no, she didn't. When the hell did that happen?"

"Just after she was surrounded by the dogs," he replied. "Did you ask her if she could identify him?"

At that, the deputy shook his head. "No, but she didn't offer anything."

"Maybe she didn't know. She's pretty traumatized over

that whole wild dog thing."

At that, the sheriff snorted. "Another reason to just shoot the damn things." And, with that, he turned toward his deputy and said, "Let's head down this way." The deputy nodded, and they slowly walked away, their guns at the ready.

Free and clear of dogs and law enforcement, or what passed for law enforcement in this part of the woods, Jenner quickly made his escape, but he deliberately walked in the direction of the growls.

If it was the wild dogs, they'd be smart to take off, but Jenner would like to flush them out anyway, if they were here. He already felt a little on the foolish side for having jumped into a tree. He just wasn't sure how his leg or recently healed injuries would handle it.

Still, if he could do what he could to save Sisco, that was a different story. Perched at the area where the War Dog had been, Jenner let out a whistle. He caught a glimpse of something dark in the greenery. He called out again, "Sisco, come here, boy."

But the dog just backed away, his eyes never wavering. The fact that Sisco even acknowledged Jenner was something. But the War Dog also saw Jenner as a threat, an enemy, and that was not good.

"I don't know what happened to you," Jenner whispered calmly, "but I've never hurt a dog in my life." Of course, if Sisco understood English, then he understood the previous conversation between Jenner and the sheriff. Sisco would also have recognized the guns, yet not necessarily knowing that they'll be coming after him and using those guns on him.

Sisco's wariness was a good thing, unless Jenner couldn't

get close enough to loop a leash on him. Something that he didn't actually have with him. Swearing at not having the foresight to come fully prepared, he realized he didn't have the dog food either. Now, however, he knew exactly who was up here, and he would be back. With a leash, some food, and a weapon.

"It's okay, buddy. I will be back." Jenner checked his pocket, and all he had was a high-protein bar. "I don't think you'll want this, but, hey, you never know. Sometimes we give this to the dogs when we're out and had no food either." And, with that, he unwrapped the package, broke it up into pieces, and threw them toward Sisco. The dog didn't even look at the food, his gaze locked on Jenner.

Jenner nodded. "I know. I'm the enemy to you, but I'm really not," he explained. Hearing the sounds of the sheriff coming back, Jenner quickly turned and walked in the other direction, back toward Kellie's place. The last thing he wanted was for the sheriff to see who Jenner was talking to and to shoot the poor dog on sight. As long as Jenner avoided the sheriff, then Sisco would likely learn to avoid him too.

CHAPTER 8

WHEN JENNER STEPPED onto the kitchen porch, Kellie was startled and then saw his face through the window, and she bolted outside. She immediately threw herself into his arms and gave him a big hug. "Are you okay?" she asked, smacking his arms and shoulders, stepping back to look at him anxiously. He was obviously surprised at her onslaught, but he replied willingly enough.

"I'm fine," he said. "And, yes, I did find the War Dog. Thanks for asking."

"Seriously?" she asked in delight.

"Yes, and it's kind of a long story," he noted. "I told the sheriff that you probably could identify the guy staying in Jim's house."

"So you did talk to the sheriff?"

"I did," he confirmed. "Did you?"

"Sure. I answered his questions. I mean ..." Then she hesitated. "Look. There's never been a good rapport between us," she admitted, "but I've tried to get along."

"Since he is law enforcement, it's always a good thing."

She nodded. "The trouble is, ... you know there's some history."

"Of course there is," he agreed, "but history doesn't mean that something like this gets pushed away."

"He didn't ask me if I could identify him. I assumed he

already knew who he was."

"I don't think he has any clue," Jenner stated.

She rolled her eyes at that. "Of course not. So, yeah, I probably should help him." She stopped, frowned, and pointed to the front of her house. "I do have a security camera up front. Didn't think of that. I probably have a picture of him."

"That's a good idea, and producing a photo of the guy could avoid you having to speak with the sheriff again. I can help you review your security tape, and together we'll try to isolate and take a couple pictures of this squatter guy and send it to the sheriff."

"Oh, I'm down for that," she stated. And then she added, "Your girlfriend—ex-wife—came back again."

"What did Laura want?" he asked calmly.

Kellie was glad to see that, outside of curiosity, there was no change in his expression. "Are you really over her?"

"I'm so over her," he stated. "Why?"

"Just ... just because she showed me a side of her personality that I actually struggled with today."

"Yes, she has a bunch of those," he noted. "I'm only just realizing how little I knew her myself."

"I think she's grown into certain aspects of her personality," she explained cautiously, "and I don't want to sound like a real bitch, but I'm not sure it's to her benefit."

"You mean, the fact that she's pregnant and doesn't want to be?"

"How did you know?" she asked, as she led the way back into the kitchen.

"She told me that she wasn't interested in having kids for a very long time and then only if there was a damn good reason for it. She didn't want to ruin her body."

"Yeah, she sounds pretty irate over the whole thing right now too," she agreed, "saying that she should have gotten a surrogate for it."

"Yeah, that sounds like her," he noted, with a nod. "We didn't actually spend all that long together, and, when we did, we weren't sharing our souls."

She nodded in understanding. "Got it, and honestly I didn't see this part of her personality before, and I've known her for a lot of years. What was she like in high school?"

"Selfish," he replied immediately, "but she's always been friendly around me."

"Do you think there is a reason behind that?"

"I have no clue," he said. "I've got nothing that she could possibly want." He frowned at that, as if considering his ex-wife in that light.

Kellie winced. "That sounds terrible, I know. I'm putting it down to a very stressful day."

"We don't need an excuse for how we feel," he stated calmly. "As long as we don't do anything to keep that gossip mill running even further amok, it's all good for me."

"Thank you. That's actually a nice way to look at it."

He shrugged. "When you've been on the bad side of gossip, it changes you. You become a little more understanding of what everybody else is doing."

"Have you ever been?"

"Sure, after she asked me for a divorce. I got all kinds of rumors, but they were rumors, and I didn't know where the truth was, so I chose not to listen to any of it and to just block it all out."

"*Hmm,* I haven't tried the mind-over-matter methodology," she admitted.

"It's probably a good thing to try every once in a while.

Otherwise you become beaten down by what everybody says. Find peace within and just avoid the noise."

"I did that for a while, and then I just focused on my son, and I didn't care what anybody said anymore," she shared. "I loved my child, and I felt true love for the first time. Although I only had him for that little bit, you are right. It's not an experience I would ever want to miss out on."

"No, of course not," he agreed, "and honestly that's a normal mother kind of thing."

"But *normal* feels like a judgment too," she stated, with a heavy sigh, "and I already had way more of that than I want to in my lifetime."

"People are cruel when they don't see you on the inside, and they only go by the outside," he explained. "I had a few people make comments about my prosthetic since I left the hospital too, and most of the time it's not very friendly. I appreciate kids that way though. They're totally honest. They want to see it. They want to know if it works. They want to know if they're talking to Superman. You know? The nice fun simple things in life."

She smiled at that. "I can see that being something that would be a lot of fun," she murmured. As they sat down at the table, she asked, "Do you want a cup of coffee?"

"No, I'm hot. I was thinking maybe …"

And she burst out with, "Lemonade."

He stared at her. "Well, I was thinking water."

She laughed. "And water you can have, but I'll make lemonade."

"So this isn't something you take out of a can, I presume." She stared at him in horror. He held up his hands. "How about you make lemonade, and I'll try it?"

"That sounds good," she said, with a laugh.

Just then his phone rang. He looked down at his screen and answered, "Jim, how's the hospital treating you?"

"It sucks. I was wondering ..." Then he hesitated.

"Speak up. What do you need?"

"Could you check on my place, please? I got a phone call from a local landowner, saying that he was looking to expand into other properties, and asked if I was interested in selling."

"I mean, that makes sense, but surely, if anybody knows about your circumstances and potentially about the break-ins ..."

Jim said, "But ... there was something odd in his tone, and I asked him what the problem was, and he told me that it looked like there had been a lot of break-ins and—as I *obviously* didn't give a crap about the property—could he buy it from me?"

"Wow, hit you while you're down," Jenner noted. "Likely thinking you'll sell it cheap."

"I have to give him the benefit of the doubt because I don't know that he actually knew where I was. He didn't ask me if I was in the hospital or had just recently been attacked," he replied.

"Let me go take a look. I didn't see anything earlier, but, hey, maybe the squatter asshole came back again. Honestly I've got to tell you that there wasn't anything for him to come back for. If he comes back for the food and the dishes, it's minor compared to the rest of the furniture that he took, but we don't want him back at all."

"No, we don't," Jim agreed. "I wish to God that I was not even here. And what shitty timing to actually get home to my parents' place only to get my ass kicked."

"Well, it won't happen again. Just make sure you're not

alone when you first return to the house," Jenner suggested, "and we can set up some security and make sure that everybody knows you're back."

"That would be nice," Jim said, "but you know how people are. If they can take advantage, they will."

"Some people are like that," Jenner agreed. "And I get it. After you've been through the shit that you've been through, and dealing with those people, it can feel like that, but people aren't *all* shits."

"Says you." Jim groaned, then added, "No, you're right. I'm just having a really crappy day right now."

"And it could get worse. Hold tight while I go over and take a look." And, with that, he hung up on the phone and told Kellie, "I'll head over to his place."

She looked at him and then nodded. "Can I come?"

"Sure, but why?" he asked.

"I don't know." She looked around and slowly wrapped her arms around her chest. "The place feels odd right now." He looked at her with one eyebrow raised, and she explained, "No, I'm not the kind who freaks out over every little thing. It's just, I don't know, there's a change to the atmosphere."

"How much did this guy like you?"

"God only knows." Her eyes went wide. "Why? Do you think he'll come back?" she cried out.

"I don't know if he's coming back to strip out more of Jim's place or to stay there because obviously Jim is in the hospital. Wouldn't take much for him to phone the hospital and ask for his room number, just to confirm. Maybe he wants his dogs."

"Well, he can have his damn dogs, as long as he takes them a long way away," she said, with spirit. Then she winced. "But you're thinking that there might be something else, something deeper, if it is him?"

"We don't know yet that anybody is back at Jim's place, so we aren't at all sure if it's our squatter or not," he stated. "So let's go see." He walked to the front door and waited, while she slipped on sandals. Then together the two of them walked to the neighbor's house.

"Where were the dogs when you were surrounded?" he asked her.

She pointed at the end of Jim's driveway. "I often go out in the evenings, just for a walk," she explained. "I'd, you know, wave, stop and talk with the neighbors for a minute or two, and afterward keep on walking, but I didn't get that far. And I have to admit I haven't been out for a walk since, … since that incident."

"Ah, hence the reason to come with me now?"

"Well, I could probably climb a tree just as well as you," she stated, "but I'm not sure beyond that."

"With two of us, it'll always be the slower person who gets into trouble," he noted, with a smile.

"And I can't do that. I will never leave somebody behind."

"You won't have a choice," he said. "When it comes to something like that, you get the hell out."

"And yet, if we run, those wild dogs will just chase us down."

"Oh, that's very true," he confirmed. "Unfortunately they're really good at running down people who stand still too." She nodded, her eyes wide. As they walked up to the property, Jenner noted, "I hear no dogs barking right now."

"And yet they were probably here," she said. "I did think I heard barking earlier. Maybe they'll stay within a few miles of this place, either looking for their owner or just staying close to what they knew as home, even if short-lived. The squatter really did a number on their heads by leaving them like that, didn't he?"

"I wonder if that intent to leave them was only temporary. I don't know," Jenner thought out loud. "It's quite possible that he thinks Jim is gone or that he killed him."

"So you think the squatter won't return because of a possible murder investigation?"

"No, not sure about that," he stated, "because, according to Jim at the hospital, this investor who wants to buy his property says it looks like there's been a break-in."

"Well, the front door is open," Kellie pointed out.

Jenner nodded. "And it wasn't this morning, but then it could easily had been the dogs."

"Right," she muttered. At that mention, she took a closer step in his direction. He offered her his hand, and she immediately grabbed on. "Thanks for the support," she replied, with a laugh.

"Dogs hunting in packs are something you should be wary of," he stated. "I'm the one who climbed the tree today."

"I bet that made you feel weird too."

"It sure did," he admitted, "but, without a weapon, that was probably the smartest thing to do."

"Right. … I guess you're used to weapons, aren't you?"

"I was when I was in navy, yes," he said. "I used to keep it on me all the time, but I don't own any now."

"And would you want to?"

"In circumstances like this, … it'd be kind of nice," he replied, "but I'm not sure I care enough."

"What will you do when you're done with whatever you're doing here?" she asked, with a sweep of her hand at the house up ahead of them.

"You mean, after I get the dog to trust me?"

"Yeah, after that," she stated. "You initially booked for a couple days."

"Yeah, we'll have to talk about that, unless you're already booked, and … there's no space."

"*Hmm*, let me check the register," she teased, with a straight face. "I might be able to squeeze you in for another night or two."

He laughed. "Make sure you can squeeze me in for a whole week."

"You think you'll stay that long?"

"I don't know. Depends how long it takes to get Jim's house in order—getting him some secondhand furniture and adding ramps where needed, expanding doorways and stuff—and I don't feel like I can leave Jim." She looked at him, startled. He shrugged. "He's got a prosthetic, like me. He's trying to rebuild his life after a major injury, like I have been trying to do," he shared. "The guy could use a little bit of help."

"Ah, so you're one of those softies," she murmured in a teasing voice.

He gasped at her in mock humor. "Don't tell anybody that," he whispered.

She chuckled. "You can hide, you know, but it won't do you any good. Your halo is showing."

He snorted. "No way I'm wearing a halo."

"Says you," she snickered. "Or is that a bald spot at the top of your head?"

His hand immediately slapped to the top of his head in shock, and then, feeling a full head of hair, he glared at her.

Kellie burst out laughing.

"THERE'S THAT SENSE of humor of yours again," Jenner pointed out, with a heavy note of satisfaction in his voice. Because he really loved it. Loved that she could joke and laugh. She was nervous, but she was here, and facing that fear was a good thing.

As they walked up to the front door, he stopped and studied it. "I want you to stay behind me."

She immediately stepped behind him. "You don't have a weapon," she reminded him.

"You know, in most other cases I wouldn't need one." Of course it was dark out and that meant predators of all kinds would be on the move.

And, with that, they walked into the house. Almost immediately an eerie silence surrounded them. He placed a finger against his lips. She nodded and shifted uneasily. He whispered against her ears, "Go home, if you want."

She looked behind her and shook her head, and he realized that it was probably scarier for her to walk out now and go home alone than it was to stay with him. Hanging on to her hand still, he slowly crept through the main living room into the kitchen. Hearing stomping on the stairs and the sounds of a man's voice, as if on the phone, Jenner straightened up and looked at her with one eyebrow raised.

She shrugged and shook her head. She had no idea who was here and on the phone.

Knowing it wasn't Jim, who was at the hospital, Jenner waited at the bottom of the stairs in the middle of the living room for the man to show up. He didn't recognize him, but then why would he? He looked like he was in his early sixties, dressed in a business suit. The man stopped and glared at him. "Who the hell are you, and what are you doing here?"

"That's a hell of a greeting," Jenner replied. "The question really is, who the hell are you and what are you doing in Jim's house?"

At that, the man's demeanor changed. "I was telling him earlier that it looked like somebody had broken into the house."

"*Uh-huh*, and that you were looking to buy it."

"Yes, I was. I mean, it's in pretty rough shape."

"Nothing that a little bit of cleaning up won't fix," Kellie added, looking around.

He snorted. "It's old and dated."

"Why would you want to buy it then?" Jenner asked.

"None of your business. Who the hell are you?" He just glared at him.

"Somebody who's concerned about Jim getting ripped off."

"Jim doesn't even live here," he snapped, with a disgusted sigh.

"I gather you haven't heard the latest then, *huh*?" And he quickly told him about the squatter.

"See? That's why a house shouldn't be vacant like this," he noted, disgust in his tone. "Jesus, he'd be better off when he sells it to me. I'll take care of it."

"Take care of it how?"

"Rentals. This town is screaming for rentals."

"I wouldn't think there was a whole lot of use for that," Jenner argued, "not a very large town."

"Nope but we're pretty close to the big city," he stated, "so a lot of people are coming out, living in places like this that they can afford, then commuting back and forth."

"Interesting," he muttered, as he studied him. "What was your name?"

"What was yours?" snapped the older man immediately.

"You're the intruder," Jenner replied, pulling out his phone and quickly snapping a picture of the man.

Immediately his face got dark and ugly.

"His name is Silas," Kellie stated. "He's married to Laura."

At that, Jenner felt everything inside him freeze. "Interesting," he murmured. "What are you doing in Jim's house?"

"I already told you," he stated, as he stepped around them. "Jesus, bloody peons here."

"Peons, *yeah, right,*" Kellie muttered under her breath, while Silas walked out the door without a backward glance. Jenner shot her a look. She shrugged. "Yeah, that's the way he talks, like everybody is beneath him."

Jenner didn't know about *beneath him,* but, wow, that guy had a hell of an attitude. As he walked back outside, he called Jim. When Jim answered, Jenner explained, "We just came over to see what kind of damage there was, and we found Silas inside, taking an inventory of what needed to be done. Are you really selling?"

"No, I didn't tell Silas that I'm interested in selling at all. What the hell?"

"He was inside, walking around. You know that that's trespassing."

"Yeah, good luck with that," Jim noted. "He's one of those rich, arrogant assholes, who thinks the rules don't apply to him."

"Well, the rules do apply to him," Jenner stated, his tone hardening, "and you do have rights here."

"Maybe." Jim sighed. "Damn. I wish I wasn't stuck in

the hospital. Is there more damage to the house?"

"No. It's a little bit messier, and I'm not at all sure that the wild dogs haven't managed to come back too. The front door was open. I don't know how Silas found it."

"Could you check?" Jim asked anxiously.

"Sure."

"The last thing I want is to have some wild dogs hanging around there when I get back again. I heard from the sheriff what a pain in the ass they are."

"Yeah, I get it," Jenner replied, "but just remember that not all dogs are the same."

"No, not all dogs," Jim agreed, "but, given my condition and the condition I'll be in when I get home, the last thing I want to do is wrestle a pack of them."

"No, you are correct about that," Jenner noted. "I'll check the locks and the lights. Do you have a key?"

"Yeah, one is hidden under the front plant pot."

At that, Jenner sighed.

"I know. I know. It was my mom's idea," Jim said. "She's always been like that."

"I'll bring you the key to the hospital. How's that?" Jenner offered. "Now that your lovely prospective buyer has already decided to walk out of the house and leave without any kind of explanation, we can at least try to secure it again."

He walked back out the front door and stood watching, taking a photo of Silas's vehicle, which appeared to be a Mercedes. Jenner couldn't get the make and model, but it was new. Silas stared at him, hard, as he drove off, giving him the finger. "Nice man."

"And our mayor, go figure. I don't think that *nice* has ever been used to describe Silas. What he wants, he gets."

"And I gather he wanted Laura."

"I think Laura wanted him. Honestly I think it's a match made in heaven." And then she winced. "Sorry."

He shook his head. "No skin off my nose." And he felt her searching gaze, as if to see the truth of his words, and he smiled. "Honest, it was a long time ago."

She nodded. "And sometimes it doesn't feel like that is long enough. She came and canceled her B&B reservation because her husband, Silas here, suddenly wanted her family—who's coming for the birth of the baby—to stay with them."

"Well then, he should be perfectly capable of hiring caterers and housekeepers and anything else that they need."

"Oh I'm pretty sure that that would all be part of it, but I don't know that Laura will feel like entertaining."

Thinking about Jim, Jenner stepped inside again and checked the front door lock, made sure it worked, quickly locked up the front of the house, checking all the windows too. Then Jenner and Kellie walked through the house, and he checked the back kitchen door. "Everything is secured. I'll come back later tonight and take a look."

"Why?" she asked.

He looked over at her. "Because some things looked like they've changed."

"Changed how?"

"It's not how I left it."

She nodded. "And you think it was Silas, or do you think it was that squatter guy?"

"I don't know who it was. At this point it could be anybody."

"Which I don't really like to think about either." She frowned, as she stared around at the room. "It's so weird to think of something like this happening here."

"Maybe, but the bottom line is, … we don't know exactly what happened, so we have to make sure we keep an eye on everything."

She looked over at him. "You are staying for a couple more days, right?"

"I am, indeed, and you'll be fine."

"I know I will be, at least at the moment. I'm not sure what Silas is all about though."

"It could be just that he sees an opportunity to buy a piece of property in town for cheap. You know? A place where all those relatives he doesn't want at his house or at your bed-and-breakfast could stay."

She winced at that. "Yeah, Silas doesn't like me."

"Oh, why not?"

"Same reason as everybody else. I was *that* girl."

He stopped and looked at her. "Seriously? People gave a crap about you having a teenage pregnancy?"

She nodded. "Apparently. I personally didn't give a crap about them, but I can tell you that Jim's family was nice to me. Everybody else was, well, … *not.*"

"Got it," he said, "and you wanted to stay in this town, *why?*"

"Because my family's roots are here," she explained, "and I guess because I feel like my son's here."

"Ah." He nodded gently. "That last part makes sense. It's hard to let go. Not sure you ever really do."

"No, you don't ever really let go," she confirmed, "and that just makes it even harder. I know there's no reason to stay close to his grave, and yet …"

He nodded. "And yet maybe one day you'll be ready."

"Or maybe not."

He looked over at her and nodded. "You're under no pressure right now anyway. You've got a home. You've got a way to make a living. You're doing things that you like on the side that are fun for you. Just keep at it. Something will break."

"Oh, it will break all right"—she chuckled—"but I don't know if it would break in the direction I want it to."

"Maybe not, but life has a habit of throwing us all these odd scenarios, and either we bounce back or we don't. I'm the kind who bounces back," he shared, "even if it takes me a little bit of time to figure out in what way. So do you."

"Oh, I don't think it took you any time at all," she argued, with a headshake. "You seem very determined to do what you want in life."

"I'm not all that long healed, which is why I didn't want to go one round or two with some wild dogs. I just wasn't sure if I would come out a winner or would end up in worse shape than before."

She winced at that. "I'm glad you didn't argue with them, and I think that many dogs are a huge problem, no matter whose they are."

"Maybe," he agreed, "but you know a lot of people can handle them just fine. I do very well with them, and I could even see doing search-and-rescue work, but I don't know. It's all in that realm of mystery for me yet," he admitted cheerfully. "Now this is locked up, and let's head back." He grabbed her hand, as they walked down Jim's driveway.

"Oh, yeah, right—lemonade," she added, as she had a bounce in her step now.

"And maybe … food?" he asked, talking to her but keeping a watch out as well.

"Food can be arranged." She laughed.

They reached the end of Jim's driveway and continued walking along the empty country road now. "Do you get a lot of cancellations?"

"Yes," she admitted. "It's kind of hit-and-miss. Sometimes, yes. There's got to be a reason why they're here, and not everybody's reasons can necessarily be locked down. You know, like the birth of a child would have been a solid reason."

"Right."

She considered that for a moment. "I would never let something like a cancellation destroy a friendship." He didn't say anything, just nodded. "And I suppose you're thinking that Laura and I don't actually have a friendship, aren't you?"

His eyebrows shot up. "I didn't say anything," he protested. "You're not getting me hooked into that. All I want to know is that you'll be okay when I'm gone." Her place was coming into view.

"Yeah, I'd like to know that too," she said, with a last glance backward at Jim's house, "but it's not your problem."

"Ah, so you're back to that? *Hey, I'm independent, and I can handle whatever comes my way.*"

"Something like that." She shrugged. "Sometimes though, it's nice to know that you're not alone."

"A *lot* of times it's nice to know you're not alone," he murmured, "and sometimes being alone is not quite what we expected."

And, with that cryptic remark, he nudged her up the steps to her B&B, and inside.

CHAPTER 9

LATER THAT NIGHT Kellie wondered about some of Jenner's comments. Seemed like he'd been through a lot—and not just with Laura. Kellie could imagine Laura being the type of person who would send a parting email with no warning. *Hey, I've filed for divorce. Goodbye.*

Laura wasn't into anything but moving up into the rich life. While her divorce from Jenner had been a long time ago, he didn't seem to see that side of her personality back then. Maybe she'd done a good job hiding it from him, or maybe—as she settled into a newer and better position financially, probably even more so with the upcoming birth of Silas's child—Laura was firmly entrenched into this *I'm doing it all for the money* role. She certainly hadn't had a problem earlier stating out loud her regret in not using a surrogate. And that still just blew Kellie away.

Funny how she hadn't seen that part of Laura either.

As Kellie sat here this evening, her laptop on her legs, Jenner came downstairs and announced, "I'll head over to the neighbor's house."

"Oh, right." She nodded. "I forgot about that."

"I don't want Jim to have no house to come back to."

She watched as Jenner headed out the door and down to the street. She wanted to go with him again, but this time it felt like she'd be in the way, and yet she didn't know why.

It was probably as much to do with running into the wild dogs as anything.

After he left, she got up and walked to the front door. Deciding not to hide inside, she walked outside and sat down at one of the big old rockers that she had on the front veranda.

As a fairly remote bed-and-breakfast, she didn't get a ton of visitors, so it was nice to have those who came by. She was a social person in some ways, although she had that somewhat blunted over the years.

She did enjoy having guests. Sometimes just people getting away from the big city or those who came out here to fish. She'd advertised at one of the local fishing clubs and had immediately gotten a couple people interested, and they came once a year.

After her recent gold-digger insights into Laura, Kellie hated to say it, but this was good money, and she appreciated their support. As she sat here, rocking in the growing darkness, she stared down the road, looking for any sign of Jenner. When she heard a vehicle brake, she jolted, but she saw no sign of a vehicle anywhere.

Frowning at that, she got up and peered into the distance, but again nothing stood out to her. Uneasy and yet not really having any reason why, she stayed quiet and then heard footsteps. Yet the footsteps were coming from the opposite direction.

She peered through the darkness at who was coming. And when she heard no welcoming greeting, she crept deeper into her veranda, where she could just watch. Whoever it was, he stood at the edge of her property, staring down the road for a long moment. He didn't say anything; he just stayed and stayed. ... That was creepy.

Kellie turned to look in the direction where Jenner had disappeared, wondering how long it would take him. When she glanced back, the man who'd been standing there, studying the road, had disappeared.

Immediately prickles of unease went up and down her spine. "What the hell is going on here?" she whispered, trying to take comfort in the sound of her own voice.

From her perspective, nothing ever happened in this town, and all of a sudden something rotten had surfaced. She just didn't know what or why—or who.

She even found herself doubting that Silas would want anything to do with Jim's property. That made no sense to her. Sure, Silas had a bunch of rentals in town, and maybe he was now focused on buying more properties outside town, but usually people bought with an idea of some return in mind. It's not like these homes were on a main road which would pull in customers for a new supermarket or even a strip mall. And, the way things were in town, those shops wouldn't want any competition, even if out here away from town.

Frowning and not liking anything about this skulking stranger, and now worried about where he'd disappeared to, she stepped back inside and closed and locked the front door. She didn't know who the hell that man had been or why he was here, but that he'd arrived and disappeared just as suddenly putting her on edge—an edge that she couldn't in any way shake off.

When Jenner didn't come back soon afterward, she sent him a text. **Is everything okay?**

He sent her a smiley face and then almost immediately sent a text and asked, **Are you okay?**

She came back with **Not sure.**

Instead of texting her, he called. "What do you mean, you're not sure?" She hesitated and then told him about the man he saw down the road. "I'm heading that way. Sit tight, stay inside, and keep the doors locked." And, with that, he hung up.

As warnings went, it was definitely not geared to keep her calm, but she sat here and waited anxiously for Jenner to show up. Then she heard a sound on her back porch. She immediately bolted to the kitchen, saw a shadow in a window, and raced to the front of the house. She picked up her phone and called Jenner, as she hid behind the front door. "Somebody's on the back porch," she whispered.

"I'm coming up the front right now. Don't do anything. Don't let him know you're there." He added, "I'll head around to the back."

She saw his shadow ever-so-slightly and watched from the living room, as he came closer. However, instead of coming to the front door, he scooted around to the back. She waited for sounds of a confrontation, but there was nothing. When a knock came at her kitchen door, she quietly came to the back of her house and peered through the kitchen window and saw Jenner. Letting him in, he looked at her and shook his head. "Nobody's here."

"Jesus, then where did he go?" she cried out, as she raced onto the back porch, looking into the darkness.

"Do you have any idea who it was?" he asked, as he put his arm around her shoulders and guided her back inside.

"No, I really don't, but I tell you that he was here. I watched him standing at the property line for a long moment or two, then lost track of him, and shortly thereafter heard him on the back porch. Then I saw the shadow in the kitchen window." Now inside the kitchen, she pointed, and he checked the window.

"And yet he didn't come in?"

"No, thank God."

"Are you sure?" he asked urgently.

She blinked at him. "What do you mean?"

"I want to be absolutely sure that he didn't come into the house."

"No, I can't be sure," she said, staring at him in shock and turned to look at the staircase.

He nodded. "I want you to stay here. I'll go up and check." And he quietly made his way up the stairs.

She really didn't want to think that anybody could have made it into the house, but it made a weird kind of sense that maybe he did. But it was also a sick kind of sense because her B&B was not the type of place where unexpected people happened to just walk inside, especially after dark.

She didn't know what was going on, but something was wrong all of a sudden.

When Jenner came down, he shook his head. "Okay, no sign of anyone."

She closed her eyes and let out a shaky breath. "What the hell's going on?"

"I need to check out the road, so again I want you to stay here, while I check."

"No." She reached out and grabbed him. "Please don't." He stopped and stared. "I don't … I really don't want to be left alone."

"I get that, but are you sure you don't want me to go find out where this guy is or even who it is?"

"Will that tell us anything?" she murmured. "This guy didn't want to be seen. He probably saw you coming from the front of the house, as he sat in the shadows."

Jenner stopped, considered it, and nodded. "And that's quite possible. I would like to ensure this guy doesn't come back again."

"You and me both," she replied shakily. "What I don't know for sure is whether it's the same guy I saw here before."

"The one impersonating Jim?"

"I mean, honest to God, I thought it was Jim. I didn't have any way to know for sure."

"And that's what you hold on to," he said, reaching out to stroke her arm. "You're doing just fine. I get it. This guy terrified you."

"And it's all wrapped up with those wild dogs of his." She shook her head. "And that's not helping. I hadn't realized how freaked out I was until now."

"No, of course not, but we will get to the bottom of this, so don't you worry."

She gave him a broken laugh. "Sure, I mean, somebody just started stalking my house, right? Although I don't even know if I would have noticed it before, except those dogs have me so spooked now."

"You would have noticed," he stated firmly. "You will sort this out. *We* will sort this out."

She smiled. "I'm really glad to hear you say that because I have no idea what the hell's going on."

"That brings me back to another thing. I asked you before what this guy was like, how he approached you, and how he acted when his dogs scared you. Can you add anything?"

She nodded. "Right, he didn't seem to be anything other than normal, until he came back that night and was yelling and beating on my front door."

"And was he drunk?"

She shook her head. "I won't say drunk, but his eyes were kind of wild."

"So chances are good he was high on drugs," Jenner muttered.

"And I gather that's bad."

"Yeah, always bad," he confirmed, running a hand through his hair. "We've got several scenarios happening here, and they're all a little bit on the odd side."

"You think?" she muttered. "I'm not sure anything about this scenario was normal."

"No, I'm not either," he agreed, "but, whatever is happening, we must get to the bottom of it."

"Right, and that just sounds like a whole lot of *Hey, don't worry*," she muttered.

He shrugged. "I do want you to be wary and alert. I want you to be thinking about who this guy could be and what he might be doing."

"But all of the options are not great." She stared at him.

He nodded. "I agree with you. Most of the options aren't good at all, but the bottom line is, if he's here because he's after you, then it's you who we need to protect. If he's here to cause trouble, then I don't know what he's after or what kind of trouble he's looking for. He could just be looking for a quick score. He already stole whatever was over at Jim's place. Maybe he's looking for something else to steal from here. After all, drug addicts are known to steal for their next hit of whatever."

He looked around, shook his head. "This is all so weird. ... If our drug-addicted squatter is looking for residential furniture, that's not normally what anybody would seek in cash-and-carry robberies. Those usually involve small electronics—laptops, phones."

She raised both hands in frustration. "It's not like I have

much."

"I know this is not a question that you'll want to consider, but have you had any creeps online?"

She stared at him and then shook her head rapidly. "I've always been very careful about keeping my identity and location private. I would never let anybody know where I live."

"Yeah, but, in this day and age, it's not all that hard to find."

"Don't say that," she moaned, "because that would just ruin everything I want to do online."

"There are some ways to keep yourself safe," he noted, "but it's that much harder nowadays. Hackers are smart and getting smarter."

"Harder is one thing. *Impossible* I'm not interested in."

He chuckled. "Got it." He looked around and suggested, "Let's go sit outside, and that might help you to feel calm."

"If you say so," she replied, with one eyebrow raised. "Honest to God, with that unknown guy just at the back door, I'm feeling mighty freaked out."

"Now that I realize he was here, I feel like I should go check out Jim's place again." She opened her mouth to immediately try to stop him and then closed it. He stared at her, asking, "What's that look for?"

"As much as I don't want you to go, and with Jim's place just a minute away, we do need to find out what's going on," she stated reluctantly.

"We do, indeed, and you know what? Depending on what I find, it will also depend on what we end up having to do. And I suppose that you don't want to call the sheriff about this, do you?"

She immediately shook her head. "And tell him what?" she asked in disgust. "He won't believe me, and he'll probably tell me how there's nothing he can do."

"Well, he probably can't do anything, but he could certainly do a drive-by and pretend to care."

"Yeah, I don't think him pretending to care will do anybody much good."

"What's his relationship like with Silas?"

"Fine"—she shrugged—"as far as I know. The sheriff likes to keep the people who vote for him happy. Silas has a lot of influence over all these lovely little townsfolk."

"You don't like Silas much either, do you?"

"I don't like any of them," she admitted bluntly, "but then my opinion could be colored from my own experiences."

"Probably," he agreed, with a headshake, "but it makes sense to me."

"And I really don't want to be the person who holds it against them," she added.

He smiled. "When you figure out how to *not* do that, maybe you should let me know."

She chuckled. "And we're back to the fact that you're one of the nice guys."

"Oh, no. That almost sounds like an insult again."

She rolled her eyes. "It wasn't intended to be."

"I'm glad to hear that. Now sit right here, and I'll be back in a minute."

"Outside or inside?"

He looked around, assessing. "Outside. If this guy comes back, you run toward me. And keep your phone on you," he added. "I'll be back as soon as I can."

She nodded, sat down at the far corner of the veranda, and waited.

JENNER PRACTICALLY RAN to Jim's house. When he got there, the place was completely undisturbed. He was afraid of that. Chances were good that whoever had been here had taken off and even now was a long way away. Sometimes that's just the way of it.

And, of course, why would anybody stay if they didn't need to? Attempted murder, stealing, squatting, his unruly dogs killing animals and scaring residents, all were things that you didn't stick around for, in case you got caught and charged for those crimes. As Jenner headed back, he heard a soft growl in the bushes. He froze, then looked at the shadow and whispered, "Good evening, Sisco. How are you doing, boy?"

He kept walking, his voice quiet. He didn't get any phone call from Kellie, and that was good. By the time he made it to the B&B, he saw her still sitting off in the corner of the veranda. "You okay?"

"Yeah, I'm still glad to have you back though."

"Good. Nothing like a nice welcome."

"And I was supposed to make lemonade earlier. And I would suggest a nightcap now."

"You're offering?" he asked, with interest.

"Sure. Why not?" she asked. "I don't keep a whole lot of booze, but I do keep a little bit for guests."

"Let's go get that drink. I'm worried that you won't sleep tonight otherwise."

"I am too," she stated bluntly. "And I need sleep."

"Anything happening tomorrow?"

"A court case." And she went inside.

He followed behind her, happy to have an end to the evening that was much calmer and more relaxed.

CHAPTER 10

WHEN KELLIE WOKE the next morning, she was surprised to feel rested and to find that she'd actually slept. She rolled over in bed, stared out at the early morning sun, and sighed. "Not quite what I expected for today, but, hey, I'll take it."

Feeling a little bit better, she hopped up, dressed for court, and headed down to the kitchen to put on coffee. She found the dining room empty and quiet, hoping to find Jenner there. While the coffee dripped, she made herself a quick bite of breakfast, put out several buns, jam, and some milk and cheese, with a note on the dining table. And then added her phone to her purse. Today would be a pain in the ass, but, hey, she needed to go.

As she was about to walk out the front door, Jenner came down the stairs and nodded. "Right, court."

She nodded too. "I hope to be back in an hour or so."

"You want to tell me what this court thing is all about?"

"I was witness to an accident," she noted, with a shrug, "I didn't want to show up, and honestly it's making me sick to my stomach that I even have to go, but I do, so I am."

And, with that, she raced out the door, leaving him staring after her. She probably should have explained more, but it was a bit of a sour spot that she even had to appear. She drove into town, made it in decent time. The process itself wasn't bad; she gave her testimony and listened to part of it. When she was told that she was allowed to leave, she stood and left. Hopefully to never return. But the distress weighed away on her.

By the time she walked back into her B&B, she sat down at the kitchen table with a heavy groan. "Thank God that's over with."

"How was it?" Jenner asked, from the dining room behind her.

She twisted. "I didn't even see you there," she exclaimed.

"Well, I am here. How was your day?"

"Fine. How was your morning?"

"Good, just doing a bunch of research. I did take some dog food to the back hill for Sisco. I just can't be sure that Sisco would get it versus the other ones."

"It's probably better if we lure them all in anyway," she admitted. "I really don't want to end up in the same scenario I was in before."

"Got it," Jenner noted. "So what was this accident you saw?"

"It was a hit-and-run," she replied. "I didn't really see a whole lot, just the vehicle."

"What was it?"

"A dark sedan. That's about all I could tell them."

"So you don't know who was driving it?"

She shook her head. "No, I don't. And I told them that a long time ago, but they still decided to bring me in."

"Of course they did, which means they really don't have much of a case. Do you know who the defendant was?"

"Some kid who they think was out joyriding, and the vehicle probably was stolen, as far as I understand from the attorneys."

"It happens. So it's not related to this Jim guy, whether the real one or the fake one?"

She stared at him in shock. "No." She frowned. "Why would it be?"

"I don't know if it is. However, I understood Jim's parents died in a car crash, coming home from visiting him in the hospital, when he first lost his leg. Then our fake guy, the squatter, seems intent on a life a crime. So I just wanted to confirm that there's no connection. And that you don't have any problems with any of your online fans …"

She shook her head. "No. I don't have anything online that makes me wary. As far as I'm concerned, everything going wrong right now is because of this squatter, pretending to be Jim."

"That's what I was thinking," he agreed. "I just wanted to hear your thoughts too."

She nodded. "And I get it. Probably a lot of shit going on around you right now, but I'm hoping that it'll calm down now." Then she stopped and looked at him. "Have you talked to Jim yet?"

"I talked to him on the phone earlier."

"How is he doing?"

"A little worried about everything that's going on. A little worried about what he'll find when he gets to his house, but otherwise he's holding pretty well."

"Is he badly injured?" she asked, with a frown.

"No, not badly, but it's a dent to his confidence for sure. It's hard to take a beating like that and just get up and walk away as if it's nothing. With a little support, I'm sure he'll do just fine."

"I hope so," she said. "I really liked his parents."

"And I think you'll probably really like Jim too," Jenner

added. "He seems like one of the good guys."

"We definitely need more of those," she stated, with an eye roll.

"We do, indeed. Now"—he rose—"I'll head out and see if I can track my War Dog again."

"Good luck. Maybe at least check to see if the dog food's gone."

"I will." He nodded. "And this time I've got my pockets full of more. I also picked up a leash and a collar for the dog."

"You really think you'll get close enough to put something like that on Sisco?" she asked.

"I hope so," he murmured. "There has to be a way to get the War Dog back again. Otherwise, well, …"

"We don't need any more people taking potshots at Sisco," she muttered, finishing his sentence.

"You're right. I'll see you later." He stopped, turned to her, and said, "I'm glad your morning went okay." And giving her a gentle smile, he left.

With him gone, she felt an emptiness that she wasn't expecting in her own home. She wandered out to the front, as she watched him leave. He lifted a hand and waved. She waved back, feeling foolish. And yet why wouldn't she wave? She really liked the man. Seemed so foolish, made her sound like a schoolgirl all over again. And that was a dangerous scenario. She hadn't experienced anything quite like that in her life before and surely wasn't ready for it now. *Definitely not now.*

As she stared around at the house that was all hers, she muttered, "You're just rebuilding your life. Absolutely no reason you can't be friendly with him though."

It's just that she knew full well that *friendly* led to other things and that led to all kinds of problems down the road. She wasn't sure she could deal with the heartache.

"Doesn't have to be that way," she said, arguing with herself.

But, of course, just because it didn't have to be, that didn't mean it wouldn't be. Sighing, she turned to do what she loved the most, especially whenever she got stressed or upset.

She started to bake.

And, with that, she set up her cameras and did a live show, her first in several weeks. So what if she was upset? Maybe somebody else could benefit from her day.

JENNER HEADED UP to the hills. He'd barely made it to the top of one when his phone rang. Glancing down, he didn't recognize the number. When he answered it, the sheriff was on the other end. Jenner winced at that.

"We're out looking for those damn dogs," he announced. "We called off the search last night, but, if you see them, let me know."

"I'm out in the back myself, looking for the War Dog."

"Well, if we find him first, you know what'll happen," the sheriff growled, his tone hard.

"And yet you don't know that Sisco has anything to do with this pack of wild dogs," Jenner argued.

"Won't matter. These dogs in packs are dangerous. Apparently they surrounded another woman in town. Her husband was coming home, driving his vehicle, and ran them off. But we can't have this happening over and over again."

"No, we can't," Jenner agreed, "but I bet it was just two of them involved."

"Yes, but a third dog was in the vicinity, so I'm sure as hell not letting that dog off the hook either."

"Did the third dog do anything?"

"I don't know. The woman was pretty upset and couldn't talk much. The husband was also fairly traumatized. They're not giving details at the moment."

"I would like to talk to them, if I can."

"You need to stay out of it."

"Oh, and why's that?" Jenner asked, his tone cool. "You and I both know I have to report back to the war department on this." At that, the sheriff stopped, and Jenner could almost hear the wheels turning in the guy's mind through his phone.

"I'll consider it," he muttered, "but we're taking these dogs out."

"You can take out the leader of the two wild dogs," he began, "but I'm not sure that the other wild dog is bad news. I know the alpha is too far gone, but the beta may be redeemable."

"Maybe, maybe not," the sheriff huffed, "but nobody here will give a shit either way." And, with that, the sheriff hung up.

Taking a slow deep breath, Jenner quickly texted an update to Badger.

Badger phoned him almost immediately. "He's really hot to kill them all, isn't he?"

"He is," Jenner responded, "and I get it. I mean, once they start traumatizing people, the locals—whether cops or the general public—will shoot to kill. From what I've seen so far, Sisco isn't anything like the wild ones."

"And that distinction won't matter, as far as everybody else will be concerned." Badger groaned. "So focus and tell me. Can you find Sisco first?"

"I'm up in the hills right now," he replied. "The War Dog seems to be hanging around these other two, but I don't think he has been integrated into the pack. The pack's pretty broken right now, after losing two of its members, and that's even more dangerous because, if these dogs are wild, they will run through town and pick up other dogs to join their pack."

"I have heard of that happening," Badger muttered. "I've never seen it firsthand though."

"The small towns are often where a whole pack would come through town, and they'll bite and force another dog in, until it has no option but to run with it. And either it survives or not. Yet it's how they increase their numbers."

"*Great*," Badger said. "Sounds like the human gang world. I hate hearing that."

"There's nothing good about wild dogs, except that they're yet another of God's creatures. It's just the way we'll have to deal with them when they go like this. And we don't even know what *this* is," Jenner admitted. "I get that the sheriff won't give a crap about a lot of things."

"No, he won't. By the way, how's the bed-and-breakfast?"

Surprised at the abrupt shift to such a mundane topic of conversation, Jenner replied, "Actually it's great."

"Have you met up with your ex-wife?" he asked, an odd note in his voice.

At that, Jenner remembered his conversations with Kellie that had focused on Laura. "No, I have contacted her, but she's been avoiding me."

"Interesting," Badger said.

Jenner frowned, wondering what his boss was up to. "Maybe not so interesting. She's eight months' pregnant with her husband's child, so there won't be any reconciliation, if you are hoping for that. By the way, Kellie at the B&B is great."

Badger chuckled. "I'm not so much sure that Kat is looking for a reconciliation as much as she's hoping that you will find peace and can move on with somebody else, somebody better suited."

"It would be the bed-and-breakfast lady, if anybody," he joked. "Even then, that's not likely to happen."

"Why not?" Badger asked.

Such open and honest curiosity was in his voice that Jenner didn't take offense. "I'm not here long enough."

"Ah, so now there's some sort of time frame?"

"No, I guess not," Jenner noted cautiously. "I really don't know what I'm doing after this."

"So leave it open. You might find out you want to stay there."

Jenner looked around, shrugged, and said, "It's a beautiful-enough countryside, but there'll have to be a reason."

"Yeah, well, the bed-and-breakfast owner might be enough of a reason," Badger teased.

Jenner thought about the woman, who, even now, awaited his return, and frowned. He really liked her, and definitely something was there, but, with everything else going on, it wasn't what he would focus on. "It would have to be something pretty special," he murmured to his boss.

"Give it a chance," Badger noted.

At that, Jenner groaned. "Stop matchmaking."

Badger burst out laughing. "Hey, when you're happy,

you want everybody else around you happy."

"I get that, but there's *happy*, and then there's *pushy*," he quipped.

"On that note, I'll ring off."

"Good idea," Jenner agreed, with an eye roll.

He had really enjoyed the bit of time he'd spent with Badger. Of course Jenner had spent more time with Kat, helping her with her prosthetic designs. She was an incredibly brilliant woman and had spent so many years and so much effort helping people like him that Jenner had been more than happy to come and take care of this job for them. Besides, any animal in Jenner's world needed the same care and love and attention that every other animal needed. Humans too.

And, when a dog had served our military, had given its life and part of its body—in this case with Sisco's damaged ankles—it made even more sense. One injured veteran helping out another. Jenner thought about that for a moment, pondering whether Sisco's damaged ankles were a part of the reason why the War Dog was hanging back. Yet Sisco didn't appear to be slowed down at all with his injuries. Not from what Jenner had witnessed.

Sisco also wasn't any less aggressive than the wild pack of dogs, when needed. However, with the other two ganging up on people and probably chickens and such, did Sisco save his energy, maybe accounting for his injuries? If so then, that could account for some of Sisco's hesitation to engage.

Jenner just wasn't sure what was going on in the animal's mind. Not that anybody ever knew things like that. Still, it made Jenner look at Sisco sideways, trying to figure out just what the War Dog's thought processes were.

As he climbed farther up the hill, urgency driving his

feet faster and faster, he was happily surprised at the way his old prosthetic was holding up. It was something that he always had to be wary of. The skin would get quite puffy if he overworked that leg on any one day or if he in any way damaged the prosthetic ankle joint. A small irritation became a dangerous sore very quickly.

Up at the next rise, he took the best vantage point that he'd already sourced out and sat down and waited. He was too far away to see if the dog food he'd left out was still there. He was going on the assumption some critter had eaten it. He just hoped it was the right one. What he was looking for was any sign of a disturbance. Depending on where the wild dogs were at, it shouldn't take too long. And, sure enough, about ten minutes later, he wondered about the continued silence and if he'd picked the right place or not.

Then he heard shouting in the distance. Immediately he stood and headed in that direction, hoping the locals hadn't gotten involved.

Once the locals got in the act, then things could get really ugly. He had to save the War Dog, first if possible. The trouble was, he just wasn't sure it was possible anymore. And Jenner wouldn't want to be the one to tell Badger that he had failed. He knew Badger wouldn't hold it against him in the circumstances going on here, but Jenner would hold it against himself. And, with that, he picked up the pace and started to run.

CHAPTER 11

WAITING WAS HELL. Kellie was still emotionally wrought from the court case earlier this morning and now was upset over what was going on around her. She decided to bury her time and attention into baking again. She already had guests coming this weekend, and they would hopefully appreciate some home-grown cooking. If nothing else she knew that Jenner would.

She hated to admit it, but she was baking more for him than anyone else. Something about the man drew her to him. *I mean, what was not to like about a man who would go to bat for a dog, who'd already suffered plenty under people's abuse.* And obviously the dog had learned from that abuse and had taken one look at the sheriff and had taken off. Or the sheriff hadn't gotten to Jim's place for that first animal check quite as early as he'd said, or alternatively maybe the dog realized a stranger was at home, and he'd taken off. Sisco could be still be hanging around, waiting for the Stippletones to return.

When they hadn't, the War Dog would have fended on its own for a while. But at what point in time would that have become a bigger issue?

She didn't know how that worked; she just didn't want to be surrounded by dogs anymore. She'd never considered herself anything but an animal lover, but the moment those four wild dogs had terrified her, she didn't want to even get involved in something that would look in any way scary.

She knew that made her a coward, but what was she supposed to do after that run-in?

She kept looking outside for any sign of Jenner. That was not good either, like she was waiting on him all the time now. It was easy to put it down as just being interested in what was happening—or even worried about this mess. But it was much more than that. She was worried about Jenner, and, being caught up with the dogs, she was worried about a lot of things. And a big worry was for his personal safety. She really liked the guy and liked that he joked around—he was one of the good ones. She didn't want anything to happen to him.

After several hours of making videos and baking, putting on laundry, getting dinner set up and ready to go, answering the phone and even a couple emails with inquiries on her bookings, she still couldn't shake off the feeling that Jenner should have been home by now. She looked down at her phone and then shook her head. "No, you're not going to text him. The man's busy. Leave him alone."

And yet nothing seemed to discourage her. At last, giving in, she quickly sent him a text and asked him how it was going. He responded almost instantly with a thumbs-up. She wasn't sure what that meant, except that he was fine and either couldn't say more or didn't want to.

She could take a hint at that. At the same time, she wasn't sure what she was supposed to do right now. Surely she could do something to help. She sent him a message, asking, **Just that to report?**

He sent back a thumbs-down emoji. She considered that and then realized, chances were, he couldn't even talk right now. Frowning at that, she thought she would phone the hospital and see how Jim was doing. And then she looked down at her cookies and smiled. Maybe she could take him something.

Quickly packing up a selection of what she'd just baked, she headed to the hospital. Maybe, if she was lucky, he would be awake and available, and she could go in and talk to him and introduce herself. She felt the need to apologize because she had assumed the other man was him. When she got to his hospital room, she knocked at his door. When she heard "Come in," she opened the door, poked her head around, and asked, "Hey, may I come in for a minute?"

"Sure." He looked at her and asked, "Who are you?"

She winced at that. "I'm your neighbor—the one who thought that squatter was you."

He stared at her and then slowly nodded. "Ah, Jenner told me about that."

"I'm so sorry," she said. "I knew your parents. ... Yet I had never seen a picture of you to know what you looked like. If I had, I would have called the cops."

He nodded. "And I wouldn't have looked like that person anyway anymore, so no need to feel guilty."

"Well, no need on your part maybe. It's a whole different story on my part," she explained, "because I do feel guilty, terribly guilty. All I had to do was make a phone call."

"I guess, when something like that happens, it's hard to shake off, wondering if you could have done something or if somehow you could have known."

"Exactly," she agreed, "and it feels like I should have known, and yet I don't know how I could have."

He chuckled. "I get it. Maybe instead of guilt you could just let it go and realize that, as soon as you did find out something, you did something about it."

"It took Jenner to get to that point though." She sighed, as she sat in the visitor's chair. "However, I did bring a peace offering."

He frowned. "Like what?" She opened the tin so the fresh aroma of cookies wafted out. His grin flashed. "You can come visit anytime. Wow, I haven't had home-baked goodies in a very long while."

"Yes, it's funny, but I think that's how most men feel, unless they have partners who actually bake," she noted. "So I brought you a selection of this morning's work."

He looked at her and asked, "You made all these this morning?"

She nodded. "When I get nervous, I tend to bake," she said, with a shrug.

"And why are you nervous?"

She explained about what was going on, and he whistled. "I knew some stuff was happening today," he shared. "I just didn't realize it was to that point."

"It is, and I know Jenner's really worried about the War Dog he's searching for, … Sisco."

"Oh, I like that name," Jim stated. "I know there were dogs around me, after my attack. It seemed like one hung around afterward too, but honestly I was in too much pain to know much more than that."

"Right. I'm sorry about that. And then, once Jenner retrieves the dog, somebody needs to look after the dog." She winced. "I'm still kind of nervous about them."

"With good reason," he noted. "I was so glazed over with pain that I don't really know what was going on with the dogs."

"Of course not," she replied instantly. "And I'm so sorry

you went through what you did."

"Hey." He shrugged. "I'm alive and well. That's what counts."

She stayed, visited for a little bit, then she got up and asked, "Any idea how long you'll be here?"

"Depends if I have a house to go home to," he stated bluntly.

She nodded. "I was in there with Jenner yesterday, checking up on it. We thought somebody was still hanging around, and we did find Silas there, doing some sort of assessment."

"Yeah, and I didn't give him permission to go in there, so ..."

She remembered that Jenner had called Jim from his house.

"I didn't realize you were there at the time," he noted, looking at her curiously.

She nodded. "Yeah, I was there. I struggle dealing with Silas."

"He talked to my parents not long ago," Jim shared. "I know he wanted to buy their place before, but they weren't interested."

"I wonder why Silas wants it though? I only know of him buying properties in town, not out in the boonies by us."

"I don't know. Something about wanting to level the house and put in a new hayfield or something." She just stared. He shrugged. "Right?"

"I mean, I know it's a farming community," she noted. "Although we have an awful lot of horses in the area, so maybe the hayfield idea makes sense. Yet he told us that he wanted your house for a weekender rental, for people getting out of the city."

"If there's any money to be made," Jim offered, "I'm pretty sure that'll be what's behind anything with Silas."

"Yes. Given that it involves Silas, that makes the most sense," she agreed. "I don't think he's the kind to let an opportunity slip between his fingers."

"No, I suspect not." Jim looked down at the cookies and grinned. "Thanks again for this."

"You're welcome. Hopefully I'll see you home soon." And, with that, she walked out of his room.

As soon as she stepped outside the hospital, she called Jenner.

He answered right away. "Hey. Sorry. I couldn't talk before. First I heard a commotion and headed that way but found no sign of any of the dogs, so I wasn't sure what was going on. Then I met up with the sheriff, who is hunting to kill any dogs he sees running loose, and we've been talking ever since." He let out a sigh of exasperation. "Now I can talk to you. So what's going on?" he asked suddenly, catching a breath.

"I made cookies this morning, and I took them to Jim at the hospital. Oddly enough, he mentioned that some dog or something hung around after he got attacked, but he doesn't remember what exactly. He heard his attacker calling to the dogs, but Jim recalls another one remaining afterward."

"Interesting," Jenner murmured. "It could be mine."

"That's what I wondered. Any chance this War Dog was just checking up on Jim? Maybe Sisco would recognize ..." She stopped. "No, that's foolish."

"What's foolish?"

"I just wondered maybe if Sisco recognized Jim as being the Stippletones' son." There was a moment of silence on the other end. "Like I said, it's foolish," she murmured. "It's not like they can sniff DNA and can recognize family members."

"I don't know about that. Dogs are incredibly smart and gifted in ways we don't always understand. However, I wonder if Jim ever saw Sisco." Jenner paused. "No, I think his parents only had Sisco like four months maybe, before they died. And that time frame means Jim was not mobile. He had had his accident, his surgery, was in rehab still, when his parents took on Sisco." He went silent again. "I'd have to check."

"I didn't even think to ask. I'm sorry," she said.

"No, that's okay," he murmured. "I can ask Jim myself. I was going to stop in and talk to him a little bit later."

"Are you staying up there for long?"

"Yes, I need to find Sisco before that gun-happy sheriff does," he noted. "I left more dog food at the same spot and saw no sign of the dog anywhere."

"Yeah, but what about any weird feeling of being watched?"

"Oh, I know Sisco's watching me," he confirmed. "I'm just not sure what he's up to."

"Is he up to anything?"

"Well, that's the million-dollar question here, and believe me. The sheriff wants to know too."

"Yeah, I'm not at all happy with the sheriff," she added in disgust.

"True, but it might be good if you two could mend some fences, as you need to be able to call him, whenever you need help."

"*Maybe*, if he ever believed a word I said. So that would mean him actually accepting that his son was the father of my child, his grandchild." She heard a moment of silence on the other end.

"Of course, if the sheriff lost a grandson and didn't even acknowledge that he had one, that might make the mending-fences job quite a bit more difficult."

"Not to mention after prom—after my supposed boy-friend failed to tell me that he had already broken up with me—I heard rumors that he had knocked up yet another girl from our high school and refused to claim her child as his either. I don't know if that was true or just rumors. I'm not even sure who the girl was. However, in the last couple years since I've been here, he got yet another woman pregnant, but he married her. So I guess he's grown up some since high school."

"Which, given you were teenagers at the time of prom, not marrying him was maybe a good thing," he suggested.

"Absolutely," she declared cheerfully. "And what I went through with Quincy? His birth father wouldn't have been the kind to stick around anyway."

"Of course, a young man not at all interested in owning up or growing up."

"No, still had to be forced into this recent marriage, as far as I understand—but maybe that's just wishful thinking on my part or just plain town gossip." He burst out laughing. "Isn't that terrible? I should be a better person."

"After the experiences you've been through," Jenner noted gently, "don't put too much pressure on yourself. Understand that, whatever it was, it came and went in your life, and you are a better person for it, and the rest will heal. If karma is out there, she'll come bite your high school boyfriend in the ass."

"I think she already did." She chuckled. "Anyway, if you're coming home for dinner, it'll still be a few hours yet."

"Yeah, I'll go back where I left the dog food," he replied, "and do one more check, see if I can actually make contact with Sisco and let him know that he is safe and okay with me."

"I'm really hoping that Jim maybe will be the answer to getting Sisco to come in."

"Why's that?" Jenner asked.

"Because I think Sisco found Jim down there, injured and on the ground. And, for all we know, then Sisco had something to do with the reason that our squatter guy called off the wild dogs."

"You think he would have left the wild dogs to chew away on a dying man?"

Kellie hesitated. "I wouldn't want to think so," she murmured, "but we have seen all kinds of things in life that we don't like and surely don't understand."

"Yeah, I don't think I like anything about this."

"Nope, and getting Jim home would be a huge benefit."

"Well, it would stop people from getting into his house," Jenner noted.

Then Kellie added, "Oh, and, by the way, apparently Silas also tried to buy the property from Jim's parents. Something about turning it into hay fields. But they refused to sell."

"Ooh, now that's an interesting bit of news. One I don't particularly like anything about. If you come up with anything else, let me know. And now I'll search for Sisco for a bit, then I'll be home. I'm hungry."

"You took a sandwich with you, didn't you?"

"Nope, I didn't. I came out without food. Well, none for me. Just food for the War Dog," he explained. "I need some quality time to just sit with Sisco."

"Good enough," she said. "I'll see you in a bit." And, with that, she rang off.

IT WAS A beautiful afternoon, but, because of the trees, it was darkening quite nicely. Jenner found a spot and just sat and waited. He saw the dog food in front of him; some was still here but not a whole lot. He closed his eyes and just calmed down his energy. Animals knew. They always knew when you were upset. They knew when you were hunting them. They knew when they were in trouble. And this one? Jenner had no clue if Sisco understood what was going on or how close he was to death by bullet.

The fact that the sheriff was out there hunting these animals was enough to make anybody's blood run cold. Once people started getting gun-happy, things could go downhill very, very quickly. Jenner was doing what he could to try to keep things calm and to keep Sisco out of trouble. But pretty soon it would get beyond Jenner's ability to change the series of events that were coming.

As he sat here, his phone buzzed. Swearing softly under his breath, he quickly pulled it out and shut off all notifications and checked the text. The sheriff sent him a question, asking if he'd seen anybody. Which meant that they hadn't located the dogs yet. Jenner wanted to smile at that, but he sent back a quick answer. **No.**

He knew it wouldn't be long before somebody would see the wild dogs because they would have to eat again. And Jenner didn't know where they were stalking down their food; it could be any number of places. He also didn't want them running through town and trying to pick up more dogs to join their pack. Two was bad enough, but, once you started getting twice that, well, it would just get uglier.

He closed his eyes and tried to calm down again. Almost immediately he heard a rustling in the woods around him. He dared not open his eyes; he also had no clue which animal it was. He did have a knife with him this time, not that that would be a great weapon of choice if he had to take down a dog trying to kill him, but it would do the job if he had to. It's just he would end up paying more of a price than he would want to if there were two of them.

He stayed calm and quiet. When he opened his eyes, an unwavering stare gazed right into his. The dog was still hidden in the trees, but his focus was right-on. Jenner took a slow deep breath. "Hello there."

Sisco didn't move.

"I know. You've had a tough couple months, haven't you? But it wasn't supposed to be like this. You were supposed to have a nice happy retirement home. Unfortunately sometimes life happens, as you well know. You were in a great place, and that changed."

He kept talking to the dog quietly, but the dog didn't move, didn't budge. And what could Jenner expect? Five minutes of talking and have the dog running to greet him and wanting a leash put on him? Not likely. The dog had been through too much already. Chances were it would take a heck of a lot more than that. It was all about patience; it was all about gaining trust.

"And I'm not so sure about your companions," he added, continuing to talk to the dog. "I suspect they've got some issues that will be hard to save them from a bullet," he murmured. "But, if I can save you, that would be something. Given a choice, I would like to save them all, but you are my priority," he noted. "So, with any luck, you haven't actually gone down that same pathway yet."

As he watched, the dog shifted ever-so-slightly. It was enough that he saw his dark coat. And he smiled.

"At least it's you," he said. "I know it's a tough life for you, isn't it, Sisco?"

At his name, the dog's ears twitched.

Jenner nodded. "And you do know your name, which means they probably kept it while they had you." Which would make sense, but not everybody liked to do that. Sometimes people got it in their head that an animal should respond to something completely different just because it was cute, completely ignoring the fact that the dog's training would be under one name. Sometimes dogs were adaptable and sometimes not even close.

He stayed for about half hour, and then, hearing another rustling nearby, the War Dog was instantly gone. Jenner turned to look off to the side, and, sure enough, it was the two wild dogs. Swearing to himself gently, Jenner said, "And now it's *you two*." Jenner still kept his voice soft.

"Not exactly sure what's going on with you both, whether you're just bad or you're just lost because you've also lost your owner. And is somebody out there, around town, looking for you? Or did the guy dump you and not give a crap? In which case I'm so sorry because this isn't the life that you expected either."

He kept his voice controlled, as the first dog, the more aggressive leader dog, got ever closer. As Jenner watched, the second dog came limping out of the woods from the right-hand side.

"Ah, and you're hurt," he stated, with a nod. "Which is also why this one is doing the hunting on my left, and you're coming up on the right side to help take down any target. Well, I'm sorry, boys. I'm not your dinner tonight." Looking around carefully, Jenner wondered where Sisco had gone but saw no sign he was even in the tree line anymore.

What Jenner needed to know was whether Sisco would partake in what was likely a coordinated attack on Jenner— or whether Sisco would stay completely separate. Watching warily, Jenner had chosen this spot specifically in case there was such an interest in what he was doing here. He didn't want to fight these wild dogs, but, once again, he found himself pinned in place by them. And he really didn't want to kill both of them either.

As he watched, the second dog came forward a little bit closer.

"You're not sure either, are you?" he asked. The dog just looked at him. He nodded. "I get it. You're hurt. You don't want to be here." The dog wagged its tail ever-so-slightly. Jenner nodded but kept an eye on the bigger, meaner one.

"What I don't know is if you're just a distraction, and, when everybody gets kind of sucked in by you, then this guy comes up from behind and takes me down." He didn't know for sure that these dogs had actually killed a human, but Jenner sure wasn't signing up to be the first. He continued to watch both carefully, talking to the second dog, seeing that he really was injured. His back leg was half dragging.

"Crap," he muttered, frowning. "Any chance I can get close enough that you might let me get beside you?" He watched as that second dog shuffled anxiously on its feet.

"You're hurting too. I'm so sorry," he whispered. As he sat here and waited, watching to see what the alpha dog would do, the injured one laid down beside Jenner. He was just far enough away that Jenner couldn't touch the dog. Yet it was also evident from the look on the poor dog's face that he was in great pain.

Jenner whispered, "I'm so sorry, buddy. This isn't exactly how you thought your life would go, was it? You had a home. You had somebody you hoped would look after you. And where that guy went, I don't know. And chances of him getting you back again aren't great. And I don't know if I'll be able to save you either, but I can try." He looked over at the first dog, only to realize he'd disappeared. At that, Jenner's blood ran cold.

"Okay, that's not good either," he whispered, slowly shifting to look around. He didn't trust that one at all. Something was going on with him, and it sure as hell wouldn't be empathy for the other dog. If the lead dog could get this poor injured one up on his feet again, the lead dog would force the beta dog to move until he collapsed. At a worst case scenario, a dog like that first one would try and hound the second one to walk some more and either eventually would kill him or would just walk away and leave him to die. And that'll have the first one running to get another pack and another meal.

Jenner just didn't know what else was on its agenda.

Once again he swore at the missing squatter, who'd decided that these animals didn't deserve any kind of a second chance—because they did. Jenner just didn't know about any such possibility for the first one now, having stalked him twice, now prepared to eat Jenner. Sometimes things happened, and the animals just couldn't be saved. And other times things happened, and you could do everything that you tried hard to do, and it just wouldn't be enough to make a difference.

He watched as the injured one whined and just kind of

rolled into place. "Sorry, buddy." Jenner continued to look around to see where the other dogs were. He saw absolutely no sign of the leader or of Sisco, and that worried Jenner even more, until he caught sight of Sisco, who stared just behind Jenner to the left. And knowing instinctively that Sisco saw something important, Jenner shifted and rather than going up a tree, he immediately pivoted to face the lead dog, coming right toward him.

The dog froze, and Jenner nodded. "Yes, you better believe it. You really don't want to be coming at me right now." Jenner cast a quick glance at the injured dog, just to be sure, but it wasn't moving.

"You're on your own now," Jenner stated. "Is that what you want? You're used to hunting in packs, and right now you've lost everybody but yourself."

The dog curled a lip.

"Yeah, I see you. You still think you're pretty tough, but, without that pack behind you, you're nothing. And this dog is injured and needs help. You? I'm not so sure about. There might be only one answer for you. Sorry, buddy. Sometimes life just does it to you, and, in this case, it'll be bad news." The dog, looked over at his partner, but seeing absolutely no action from the injured dog, the alpha dog immediately backed up a few feet and then, with a bark, took off.

Feeling a sense of relief, Jenner looked over to see that Sisco had also disappeared, as if not trusting the other dog. Jenner just hoped Sisco wasn't anywhere near the alpha when the sheriff found that one wild dog in particular.

As Jenner approached the injured beta dog on the ground, he called out to him. The dog whined. "Yeah, I hear you. However, circumstances and all that, I just don't know if it's safe to trust you." He bent into a crouch position and just watched. The dog whined again, his tail trying to wag. "And the other dog that I saw, you didn't have your heart into killing, like he did, but not many people understand that. When a wild dog pack like that is formed, either you survived or they would often kill you, if you couldn't keep up." He'd seen it time and time again, and, in a case like this, he could only hope that this dog would get a second chance.

He phoned Kellie. "Do you know one of the local vets?" he asked.

"There is one in the next town over," she said, "and a retired one here nearby too, now that I think about it."

"Maybe the retired one then," Jenner said.

"Did you find Sisco?"

"I found Sisco and two of the wild dogs that I think went after you, but this one's hurt." She hesitated. He continued. "I know. Believe me. I know, but I think this one deserves a second chance."

"You know nobody else will agree."

"No, particularly the sheriff. However, I think, now that this one's been separated from his buddy because of his injury, the lead dog is likely to go after his next victim on his own, and I don't know, maybe hook up with some other dogs if he can. I can't be sure what's on its agenda. These dogs are lost. They had somebody, and now they don't. And they need to be fed."

"I get it," she replied. "I do know the retired vet quite well. I'll give him a quick call and get back to you."

And, with that, he hung up. He wished that she would stay out of it, and he could have just contacted the vet himself, but he understood her need to help. And also that need to distance herself from these dogs.

"You really got yourself a bad reputation," Jenner told

the injured dog.

The dog whined again.

Jenner took several steps closer, and, just as he went to crouch beside him again, Jenner heard the other dog growl right next to his ear. He froze for a second, then turned to see the alpha one that he had hoped had run away. Nope. He stood within three feet, his lips curled in a horrible grimace, the sound not soothing that came from the dog.

"Yeah, I get it," Jenner said. "You don't want me touching your friend. But, at this point in time," he murmured, "I'm not sure what your motive is. And this guy needs help."

He stayed in between the two dogs—hoping that the injured one was really injured, and it wasn't some kind of ruse. He'd seen animals play all kinds of games. Yet it looked like the other animal was slowly collapsing into unconsciousness.

The lead dog barked, and he took two steps closer. Jenner could almost feel its breath on his face. The dog was waiting for something; Jenner just didn't know what. And maybe the leader was waiting for his buddy to get up and to give him a hand. Jenner risked one more glance but was relieved to note that the other dog was definitely out cold. He told the lead dog, "Sorry, this guy is too hurt. You're on your own now."

Jenner studied him closely. "You'll have to decide what you'll do now." And Jenner waited. Just when he saw the other dog's legs bunching up for a frontal attack, a flurry happened behind Jenner, and suddenly the lead dog was hit full-blown in the chest, hard, by something black. The alpha dog bounced off the ground, spun around, and was all teeth and fury and howls, before it was suddenly over.

One dog took off, and, standing beside Jenner, all alone, was Sisco.

CHAPTER 12

KELLIE QUICKLY PHONED Jenner back. When he answered, she said excitedly, "He says he'll take a look at the dog."

"Good. I need to contact the sheriff in a bit too."

"Why's that?" she asked, frowning. "He's hardly anybody I want you to be talking to."

"No, but I just had an altercation with all the dogs." When he quickly explained, she sat back in her chair in surprise.

"What? Sisco actually knocked the other dog away?"

"Yes," Jenner confirmed. "He's done that before."

Such pride was in his voice that she had to laugh. "He's hardly your dog."

"I know," Jenner admitted, "but I'm a patriot, and this dog's been very well trained, and, in this case, I think it's even more than that. He knows the other dog's rules of the wild, but Sisco chose to protect me, and that's important," Jenner said. "I also have the third dog, which is the one wild one that I was hoping to save, that you called the vet for. I think I can lift him and carry him down to your house. I don't know whether I'll be able to bring in Sisco in at the same time. He's already taken off, but I know he's not gone far."

"Why do you think he's taken off?"

"You know what? A part of me hopes it's because he's trying to keep track of the wild dog, the leader of the pack. Sisco knows he's dangerous and is going against everything Sisco's been trained to believe in."

"You give an awful lot of human qualities to this animal," she noted cautiously.

He took a deep breath. "I know, and I get that nobody else would understand, but anybody who's seen Sisco in action and realizes how well trained these War Dogs are and how devoted they are, you wouldn't have these doubts."

"And of course I haven't had any of that," she noted, "and neither has the sheriff."

"I know. That's why I want to see if we can get this other dog looked at first, to see if it's even worth trying to get him back to health. He is injured. I just don't know how badly."

"Well, bring him down," she said. "It's not like I give a shit what the sheriff says anyway."

"And I don't want to cause any trouble between you and the sheriff," he stated instantly.

"You haven't caused any trouble, any more than he's already brought on himself," she declared. "Once an asshole, always an asshole." And, with that, she hung up.

He had been a jerk to her for a long time. She presumed he was that way with others around town. She didn't know. But he favored his son of course. And Silas. Certainly no love was lost between her and the sheriff. She didn't call him whenever there was a problem, although she might have had to if this problem with her squatter hadn't stopped.

She'd had more than enough dealings with the sheriff over the impersonator. And it's not like the sheriff had run the fake Jim to ground either. Although, if she wanted to phone the sheriff and find out, it wasn't an issue. Or it shouldn't be an issue.

Anyway, first she had to get this injured dog to the vet. She hated to think that it had been involved in any of these issues around town, but she couldn't be sure. She knew she would recognize it, and she also knew that the one that had been the most dangerous had been the other one, the one who ran away. Well, she hoped it was the other one. Again she didn't know.

She stepped out on her back porch to watch, and, sure enough, in the distance, she saw Jenner moving slowly, and then she winced, as she realized his leg was bothering him. But he was also stubborn enough that he wouldn't say anything or do anything to help it right now. She swore, as she watched him slowly navigate down the hill, but no way she would run up there to deal with a very injured dog. Not with the alpha dog still loose.

When Jenner got closer, she yelled, "Take him right to my car." He nodded but didn't say a word. She looked for evidence of strain on his face, but, true to form, he wouldn't give away anything by saying he was in pain or by asking for help. Not right now anyway. He was focused on the dog.

As they got closer to her vehicle, she asked, "Are you always this stoic?"

He laughed. "Not necessarily, no, but there must be some understanding of where the pains starts and stops," he noted, "and, for me, that time has come and gone. I'm just in pain now."

"From the injuries, your leg?"

"He's heavy," he stated succinctly, "and that's a given, no matter how injured you are. None of this has to do with my injuries."

She didn't say anything to that, but she didn't believe him.

He smiled. "Let's just get the dog to the vet."

And, with him holding the dog in her passenger seat, she buckled up her seat belt. "What do you think about the War Dog?"

"I'm impressed and thrilled, and I really hope I can save him," he said fervently. "I know it sounds stupid, but it really feels like maybe he's looking to keep an eye on the wild dog and to save whoever it is that the wild dog's going after."

"And yet you know that that'll only go so far."

"I know. It'll be a hell of a fight, if it ends up that way," he noted, "and I don't need to tell you how dangerous it'll be for anybody around it."

"I know," she whispered. She took one look at the dog and asked, "You okay to hold it?"

"I am. It's unconscious."

"Yeah, but that doesn't mean, when I start up the vehicle, that it won't get upset."

He looked at her and suggested, "You don't have to drive me."

"Yeah, I do," she stated. "That dog you have is the one who kind of held off at the back of the pack and seemed to need to get pushed into being mean."

"In these wild packs," Jenner explained, "it'll often be a case of, if you're weaker, you have to do what the other one says."

"And that's the same no matter what, whether human packs or animal packs," she noted. "So my sympathies are with this one." And, with that, she started the car with a wince, then checked the dog, before driving slowly but carefully toward the retired vet that she had known since she was a kid.

They arrived shortly. When she hopped out, the front door of the house opened, and the vet came out, looking at her. "It's quite nice to see you," he said, by way of greeting. And then he took one look at the dog in Jenner's arms and frowned. "Is that one of these wild dogs that has been hunting people?"

"Yes," Jenner admitted, "but I don't think this one is choosing it."

The vet nodded. "Still, if they get a taste for blood ..."

Jenner nodded. "I figured we should come see if he could even be saved."

"And then you have to ask yourself if it's worth saving."

"Every animal's worth saving if we can get it rehabbed," Jenner stated. "And, honest to God, I'm not at all sure that this one deserves to die. Bad beginnings and all that."

"Bad beginnings can still cause all kinds of trouble."

Jenner wouldn't argue with the vet, but he carried the dog inside and wasn't surprised when the vet had Jenner put the dog on the kitchen table. If this was a retired vet, he didn't have proper exam rooms or a clinic.

While the dog was still out, they quickly put a muzzle on him, so that, even if he did wake up, they could control it somewhat. And now, with a collar around its neck and a lead then attached, the vet noted, "I feel a little bit safer."

"I know," Jenner agreed. "I have to admit that I was a little hesitant to pick him up."

"And what's this about a War Dog?"

He looked over at Kellie, and she shrugged. "I had to explain who you were and why it was important."

"Right." Jenner gave the vet a shortened version of it.

"Well, I'm glad to see the war department is giving a

crap about these guys. It's sure a lot better than what we did to the poor animals in the Vietnam War," he said. "That would be a stain on our history forever."

As he kept working on the dog, he mumbled, "It's got a broken right leg. I'm not seeing necessarily anything major. No swelling, no bleeding outside of the leg," he noted, "but lacerations are all along the hip and the side, and that could be from anything. Also fairly rough shape."

"As expected." Jenner nodded.

"It's kind of an odd circumstance. I'm not sure what we actually have here. At the same time, we can't really take a chance on it being something more."

Jenner wasn't sure what that meant, but, if the vet were willing to give them a hand, Jenner was more than willing to take care of whatever they needed in order to make this happen. "I'll cover whatever the dog needs."

At that, the doctor looked back at him and said, "We might need surgery on that leg. And I'll have to do a pretty thorough exam to avoid it. The responsible thing would be to take it to an active clinic though."

"And you're right," Jenner agreed, "but I also know that the sheriff is gunning for this dog."

At that, he asked, "Why?"

"Because he's part of the hunting pair of wild dogs, and the sheriff wants to kill both of them."

"Of course he does," he said, with a heavy sigh. "Like I haven't heard that a time or two. You also know, in many circumstances, it's probably the better idea."

"Absolutely," Jenner replied, "but I'm not sure that this animal is the one that needs to be put down."

The vet nodded, considering his patient. "I can set the leg. The break looks fairly clean. I don't know about any internal injuries. The dog's pretty bruised and beaten up."

"And I suspect that's from the other dog, the more aggressive leader dog," Jenner suggested.

"Yeah, I've seen that a couple times in my career, when they're coming into town, looking to grow a pack or to fight somebody into submission. There's been a couple cases of that brought to me over the years." The vet shook his head. "As much as I love Mother Nature, sometimes she's a complete bitch."

"It's all about the strongest surviving," Jenner noted. "And this one is nowhere near strong enough to survive against the other one."

"And what about your War Dog?"

"Sisco is standing up to the wild dog, the leader of the pack. I'm kind of hoping that we can find Sisco a good home after this, where he'll be safe and where he can go back to spending his days as a pet. Same as this one."

"You'll need somebody who can handle the well-trained dog and also a dog gone wild."

"I'm not even sure who the guy is who left these dogs behind. For all I know, he's coming back for them."

"You'll let him have this one?"

"Well, since he's wanted for squatting at Jim's place, knocking Jim unconscious, then stripping Jim's house of everything, leaving Jim out there to die," Jenner explained, "*hell no.* I'll toss his ass in jail." And that, of course, necessitated another series of stories.

KELLIE THANKED THE retired vet for his help, giving him a big hug.

The vet was already hooked on trying to save the animal, as best he could. He asked, "Do you want me to report it to the sheriff?"

"You do what you feel like you have to do," Jenner said. "My preference would be no. Not at the moment. I'd like to get Sisco in my custody first. Plus let's see how this dog heals as well."

He nodded. "I'm not required to report him," he stated. "However, I am warning you that, if the dog gets dangerous, I will not be able to keep him."

"No, of course not." Jenner hesitated and then asked, "Would you let me know?"

"Yeah, I would let you know first." The vet frowned at the dog. He adjusted the IV he'd hooked up and said, "You're lucky that, after I sold my practice, I still ran a clinic out of here. So I just couldn't let this dog go when I knew I had the wherewithal to help."

"Which is also why I knew to call you," Kellie said, from his side.

He nodded. "Sometimes I wonder at what point in time we're supposed to stop doing what we do."

"Maybe never," Jenner admitted. "When you think about it, we are who we are on the inside."

She looked over at him, smiled, and nodded. "Good point."

The vet smiled and then looked at Kellie. "Looks like you found yourself a decent young man this time."

She flushed, her eyes widening. "He's hardly mine," she replied in a dry tone.

The vet just nodded. "Says you. Anyway I'll let you know first thing in the morning how he did overnight," he stated. And he waved them off.

Leaving the dog in his hands, Kellie got back into the car, more embarrassed than she knew what to do with.

"Don't worry about it," Jenner said. "I've certainly heard worse things."

She looked over at him. "Well, it was a compliment to you. However, it was yet another ding against me."

"And I don't think he meant it that way."

"No, it's his generation. I also don't really think he thought about what he was actually saying," she murmured.

He chuckled. "I guess for some of these guys, it's hard maybe even for them to care about what they say or how they say it. They're blunt. They say what's on their mind, and they move on."

"And I'm okay with that honesty," she noted. "Still, it'd be nice if people would forgive and forget."

"And yet you stayed here."

"I did. It's my home. Why shouldn't I?"

He nodded. "And it's a beautiful home in a very nice countryside."

"And what will you do," she asked, "when you get this all dealt with?"

"I'm not sure," he replied, looking at her. "I might stay for a day or two."

She raised both eyebrows. "Really?"

"Yeah, maybe," he noted, with a shrug. "I mean, obviously I'll just extend my reservation, if you have room," he added, with a sudden frown.

"I have room." In her mind, she made a mental note, determined to find a bedroom for him, one way or the other. "And it would be nice if you stayed. It's been good to have you around."

"Well, let's hope it's not just for keeping you safe," he

said, with a chuckle, "because, so far, I haven't done well in that department."

"It's not your department to take care of me either," she noted.

"No, maybe not," he replied. "And more than that, I know that you're perfectly capable of taking care of yourself."

And for some reason, those words alone brought a flush to her cheeks. "I don't think I've ever had anybody give me a vote of confidence as to my ability to take care of myself," she shared, as she drove home. "Such an odd feeling."

"Why's that?"

"Most people probably just say it's up to you to take care of yourself, and I have done an okay job at it."

"I think most people are probably assuming that you *can't* take care of yourself. A lot of people, once they go through something like you've been through, they struggle with reality afterward. I'm certainly not criticizing them. I just know that life can become that much harder."

"Oh, I agree," she stated, "and honestly, if I hadn't been through what I've been through, it would have been really hard sometime to understand what I was supposed to do now. Instead I just took it as one of those lessons in life, and, well, I've continued on by myself in that direction since."

He looked at her, startled. "You haven't had a boyfriend since?"

She shook her head. "No, once you realize how easily that can go south …"

"There is such a thing as birth control."

"I know, and that wasn't the issue. It was more about what happened later, when the shit hit the fan."

"Right, so it's not even about physical relationships. It's more about trust."

It was her turn to be startled. She looked over at him and nodded. "You know what? You may be right. I never considered it."

"Well, that would be my take on it, but what do I know? I haven't had any serious relationships since my wife sent me that email, telling me that we were done and that she was divorcing me. At the time, she told me that she would marry my best friend. Only, when I confronted him, I found out they weren't planning on getting married. I don't know who she was talking about back then because it wasn't Curt, and maybe Silas came later."

"And maybe she just used Curt as an interim excuse or to deflect from her decision to marry an old rich guy."

"Maybe, I don't know. I did ask Curt about it. And he said, yeah, they had an affair, which was enough of a reason for me to kick his ass into tomorrow anyway," Jenner noted. "However, they certainly weren't getting married, and he had not fallen for her, and he was pretty ashamed of himself. As it is, he's no longer my friend because, well, again, *trust*."

"God, that's terrible," she said. "Especially when you're overseas in the service."

"And, of course, that's when most of these things happen."

She nodded. "I've heard all kinds of horror stories. It sucks."

"It does, especially if you're the one getting ditched," he admitted. "I thought we were partners for life. And apparently we were partners *until* she found somebody better."

Kellie winced at that. "And maybe she's happy now."

"I hope so," he said. "I mean, I can't hang on to that crap. I wouldn't even have tried to contact her, except that my boss's wife, Kat, was of the opinion that I might need to deal with something."

"And was she right?" Kellie asked curiously.

"I'm totally okay with whatever Laura does, so maybe it was the right thing to have tried to speak to her. At least this way I don't have to even think about it anymore."

"I kind of like the sound of that," Kellie admitted. "It frees you up to having a relationship."

"Which is something, like you, I hadn't really worried about, specifically not in the last several years."

"Good," she noted, with a cheerful smile. "That means we're both single and available, and who knows?" She chuckled. "Maybe you'll just stick around so we can get to know each other."

He flashed a grin her way. "I tell you what. Those cookies of yours alone are deadly."

"Aha, so you'd only be interested in my baking," she teased, with a knowing gaze. "Well, at least I know what the exchange is upfront."

At that, he burst out laughing. "Wow, you know that your cookies would be tempting, but I would never enter a bargain for you so lightly."

She chuckled again. "Well, how about no bargain? How about we just spend a bit of time together and enjoy finding out more about each other?"

"Oh, I'm all for that," he agreed, looking at her in surprise. "I certainly thought that you would have had somebody else in your world."

"Nope. Remember that whole trust thing?" She hesitated. "Will you still be okay to stay? Even if your ex comes around again?"

"She's bound to," he stated, "and so is Silas."

"Why's that?"

"Because I put a bug in the sheriff's ear about Silas wanting to buy Jim's property and trespassing while Jim was in the hospital."

"And is that a problem?"

"No, not necessarily. The sheriff just seemed surprised at that information though. And I also made mention that I wouldn't take kindly to anybody hassling Jim until he had a chance to actually settle in and to decide whether or not he would stay permanently."

"Right, and you know Silas is the kind to hassle him."

"I definitely got that impression," he murmured. "And just as I'll be here as an advocate for the dog, I'll definitely be an advocate for Jim." She looked over at him. "Been there, done that. I know how hard it is to rehab a missing limb. Now he's also dealing with the loss of his parents and his anger over the beating he just took."

"I don't know what you've got planned for your life," she began, "but, if you'll become an advocate for veterans, why don't you make it official?"

He stared at her. "What do you mean, make it official?"

She shrugged. "Surely there are departments or groups or, I don't know, even private people who help people like Jim."

"Maybe," Jenner agreed, with a shrug. "I don't know either. I haven't really looked into it."

"I'm not sure you've looked into your future at all, have you?" she asked. "Somebody asked you to come help out with the War Dog, and you came running."

He nodded. "I was helping Kat with the testing of some of her prosthetics, but locating these War Dogs is hardly a paying position. Although it could be. I do love the field."

"Nice to know you don't have money worries," she noted in a teasing voice.

"Well, they're paying for my accommodations here," he admitted, with a shrug. "I don't get paid for my time, but I'm fine with that. I'm doing this because I want to."

She nodded. "And that just adds to that whole nice-guy persona that you're trying to keep hidden."

He snorted. "Don't tell anybody, will you? You'll ruin my image."

At that, she burst out laughing, liking him more with every moment that passed.

CHAPTER 13

J ENNER ATE ANOTHER fantastic dinner prepared by
Kellie, yet she didn't seem able to accept a compliment.
Once he started eating her salmon in a sauce and the roasted
potatoes, he couldn't stop. He looked at his empty plate,
sorry to see it was all gone. "That was divine. Did you ever
think about opening up a restaurant?"

"Oh, good Lord, no. I would want to do things on my
own timing, not on a restaurant's clock," she explained, with
a chuckle. "But thank you. That is a compliment."

"Seriously, you're a wonderful cook." She looked pleased
at the compliment, but he didn't do it to compliment her; he
meant it. If he could get a hold of this kind of food all the
time, man, he would be one happy puppy. Just the thought
of having somebody around who could cook like that was
enough to make him smile.

She asked, "What'll you do now?" She rose to clean up
the dishes.

He hopped up immediately to help, ignoring her pro-
tests. "I'll go back up the hill and take another look for
Sisco," he said, "and then I'll come down in the dark and
check on Jim's place." She froze and looked at him in worry.
"I know. It's not something you want me to do, but I need
to make sure that nothing is going on over at Jim's place.
That man needs his home."

She nodded. "What if he decides to sell though?"

"I didn't hear anything in his voice that said he wanted to. I think it's more a case of he feels like he can't live on his own. That was just my impression. I'm sure that beating he took really did something to him emotionally."

"It's psychological," she agreed. "For that, I'd like to give that squatter guy a good old beating myself."

"Well, you just hold on to that thought," Jenner said, smiling, "and we'll see what we can do, if and when we ever catch this guy."

She chuckled. "I hope to God I never see him again."

"Even better because you're right. It's way better to not even see this guy ever again."

She nodded slowly. "There's nothing nice about him. He was just kind of freaky."

"And you haven't seen him since?"

"No, not since then. I think he basically was checking to see if I had people here. And the fact that you're here has likely chased him away."

"Well, I wouldn't trust him regardless."

"No," she murmured. "I wouldn't either."

"Maybe we'll get to the bottom of that too."

She looked at him curiously. "What? You'll just try to solve everybody's problems?"

He shook his head, as he smiled at her. "Hardly, but, if I can solve a couple of them, then I'm happy to do it."

"You are pretty special to not only go out of your way not only to help a stranger like Jim but also to help him several steps beyond just normal everyday type of help."

Jenner shrugged, wondering if maybe he couldn't take a compliment either.

"Will Jim be in a wheelchair?"

"For a while, yes. He still needs to get a decent prosthetic, but he's on crutches right now. I don't know that his amputation is good enough to handle his current prosthetic, so the easiest answer for him to start is a wheelchair. And then we'll have to see what we can do."

"But his house isn't wheelchair accessible, is it?"

"No, and I think that's always in the back of his mind, and I don't know if Jim has any money to do the necessary modifications."

"There should be funds for veterans for that," she stated and then frowned. "You know what? I thought the parents had some money, but I do remember how she was worried about stocks having collapsed."

"Right, and that would be something that Jim will have to look into, once he gets all settled. And that'll be hard on him too."

"Of course it is, but it's not impossible. Meaning that, if you are here to help him out, he can do just fine."

He hesitated and then said, "I guess it did sound like that, didn't it? I didn't mean to sound so arrogant," he admitted. "I just know that, with support, people can do all kinds of things."

"And I agree with you. I just don't know if Jim'll get the kind of support he needs. He's dealing with emotional and psychological traumas, as well as physical healing."

Jenner frowned and went really quiet.

"And I get it. You can't help everybody."

"No, but I do have a unique set of skills that maybe I can help some people. Then maybe I can do referrals for other things. I'll have to give it some thought."

"You do that," she suggested, smiling.

He looked over at her suspiciously, but she ignored him.

185

THE FACT THAT Jenner was even talking about being around a little bit longer thrilled Kellie to absolutely no end. She really liked this guy, and everything that he did or said just added to it. She smiled at him. "I was just thinking that you're one of the real heroes."

"Oh, don't even start down that pathway," he replied in horror, staring at her. "That puts expectations out there that I might not be capable of seeing through."

"Good point," she admitted, "but it still won't change my opinion."

He snorted. "In that case I'm heading out there, so I can get away from you and your rosy view of life." He chuckled. Then he stopped and frowned. "But you haven't really had any chance to have a rosy view of life, have you?"

"No." Then she laughed once more. "But I wouldn't have missed any of it."

"So your theory right there doesn't work." He rolled his eyes. "You'll find out that I'm just like everybody else, human."

She nodded. "Absolutely. I'm just really glad to have met you." She walked over, gave him a hug. "Please take care." Then she reached up and gave him a quick kiss on the cheek.

He held his hand to her cheek for a long moment, just staring at her.

"Oh, did I cross some kind of a line?" she asked, worried, as she stepped back.

"Absolutely not, … but, if you want to give me a kiss, you need to make it a *real* one."

And, with that, he took her in his arms and laid one on her.

JENNER STEPPED BACK, observed the glazed look in Kellie's eyes and her lips pouting still, as if waiting for a second kiss, and he murmured, "That's much better."

And, with that, he let his arms slide off her and stepped out into the growing darkness behind the house. He immediately raced toward the spot where he had left the dog food and saw that most of it was gone.

"Good," he noted. "And I don't know which one of you took it, but that's fine. Either way it would save another life tonight." *And hopefully calm some of this down.* And then he moved away slightly and sat down in the darkness.

He called out several times and then just sat here peaceably. When he heard a rustle behind him, he smiled and said, "Hey, how's it going?"

He wasn't sure there would be any answer, but he was just happy to sit here and wait. When the noise turned to a growl, he swore. "Is that you eating the dog food? I was hoping I wouldn't have to deal with you tonight. I've already got your buddy at the vet's. No guarantee that it'll be something you're happy about though."

He had been waiting for Sisco. Instead he got the wild dog. He didn't show himself, but the growls continued. He didn't show, didn't show, and then finally stepped forward ever-so-slightly. Jenner nodded. "Yeah, you're not the one I was looking for, but, hey, I guess that's what I get for putting out dog food for anybody. And you're right. You are welcome to it," he said in that same conversational tone. "Now where is Sisco?"

At that, hearing his name, Sisco appeared on the far side.

"You're just watching this one, bud? You know that I'm

glad to see you. I'm hoping you'll keep this guy off my back." His phone rang just then. He swore at it because, of course, he hadn't shut it off. He pulled it from his pocket and hit Talk, without losing sight of the other dog. "Yeah, what's up?"

"It's the sheriff. You find those dogs?"

"I saw them in the distance," he replied, swearing silently. "Why, what's up?"

"We haven't found any sign of them," he said in disgust. "It's like all three have taken off."

"Well, I'm pretty sure they've got places to hide." *What has the alpha dog done now?*

"You mean, outside of killing chickens?"

"Can anybody prove it was them?"

After a moment the sheriff replied in anger, "Don't tell me that you've gone all goody-goody on me now?"

"I was always on the dogs' side," he murmured. "I don't want to see any animal killed unnecessarily."

"Well, you heard what happened to Kellie. She got surrounded by them."

"Sure, but that doesn't mean that they weren't any more dangerous than that. Yes, that's bad enough," he admitted, "but I'm not sure that that's something that you should shoot them over, is it?"

"Sure is. They don't have any owners."

"Yeah, where is the hunt for that guy, by the way?"

"No sign of him," he announced.

"Well, that's crap.'

"Besides, I don't think Jim should be too worried about losing all that old furniture. It just saved him trying to get rid of it now."

"Why would he be getting rid of it?"

"Because he's selling the house to Silas," the sheriff stated, a note of confusion in his voice.

"I didn't hear that from Jim," Jenner stated, staring down at his phone and then immediately raising his gaze to make sure the alpha dog was keeping its distance.

"Generally Silas gets what Silas wants." The sheriff laughed. "The house isn't ready for Jim anyway. So it'll cost more money to fix up than it's worth," he said, with a snort.

"Maybe, but that doesn't mean Jim'll get enough by selling that house to move on and to buy another house with the proceeds either."

"No, and Silas won't pay top dollar for a piece-of-shit house like that either," the sheriff replied. "Why would he?"

"Well, I don't know that Jim's actually selling it. Do you?"

"I told you. Silas gets what Silas wants."

"Maybe not this time," Jenner murmured.

"Oh really? You'll go to bat for Jim now?" he asked, with disgust. "You're just a regular little do-gooder, aren't you?" And that was the second time in just the last couple minutes that the sheriff had called Jenner something like that, and not in the nice way that Kellie had said the same thing. Jenner felt some anger jarring his stomach toward this sheriff. "If ever anybody needed a hand right now, it would be Jim."

"Sure enough, but I mean Silas *is* giving him a hand, offering to buy that piece-of-shit property."

"It actually looks like a nice piece of property to me," he argued. "And his parents loved it."

"Sure, they've also been there thirty years, paying basically nothing for it. Now at least Jim would get some money out of the deal."

"Why would Silas even want it?" Jenner asked curiously.

"No clue. Doesn't matter. He's buying up all kinds of properties around town. Going to make a fortune off whatever plan it is he's got going." The sheriff snorted. "Doesn't matter to me one way or another."

"Of course not," Jenner noted, with a faint sigh. "I guess he contributes nicely to your votes too, doesn't he?"

"Hey, if you're implying that something untoward is going on with Silas," the sheriff replied, "you're wrong. He's a good man."

"Is he? Well, let's hope that he listens when Jim says no the next time."

"Well, Silas has nothing to do with it then. If Jim says no, Jim says no," the sheriff stated. "There's nothing sinister about this at all."

"Good, I'm glad to hear that," Jenner noted, "because the last I talked to Jim, he didn't want to sell."

"Pretty sure he changed his mind though," the sheriff added. "Maybe you should worry about yourself. You're only here for a little bit longer. I wouldn't want to see you get too messed up in anything." And, with that, the sheriff rang off.

Jenner stared at the phone. "Was that a threat?" he said out loud. When he heard a growl in response, he looked up and said, "Yeah, I hear you." This time, it was just Sisco. The other dog was gone.

"What are you doing here, Sisco? Like, is there some rhyme or reason to this? The other dog took off presumably because he's not hungry, but what is your job in all this? Please tell me that it's a good role because anything other than that, and I'll have a really tough time keeping your ass alive," he muttered.

At that, Sisco barked and took off.

"Well, damn. That's not helpful." Giving up for the evening, Jenner headed toward Jim's house. Stepping inside and taking a closer look around, he still thought it was a nice house. It could be a great place to live, with some basic modifications. And it'll be a really good place for Jim. Considering all that, Jenner found himself already heading for his truck, wondering if he should go to the hospital.

Pulling out his phone, he contacted Jim at the hospital and asked, "Hey, have you decided to sell?"

"No," Jim said. "Why?"

Jenner relayed what the sheriff had said.

"Of course Silas said that," he replied, with a hard sigh. "You know that it won't really be an easy place to live."

"It won't be a bad place though either. I was just looking at the house. It won't take much to do some simple modifications to it." When Jim went silent, Jenner asked, "Jim?" Hesitation filled his voice when he said, "You there?"

"Like how much? I don't have any money."

"But you do have a home," Jenner noted.

"And maybe if I sold it, I could move to a place that was already modified."

"How much did he offer you?"

When Jim shared a ridiculously low sum, Jenner winced. "Do you really think you'll go anywhere with that kind of money and buy anything comparable?'

Jim thought for a moment and agreed, "No, you're right. I'm not, am I?"

"No, you're not," Jenner confirmed. "As much as I'd like to see you settled someplace where you'll be okay, I don't want you to just accept some cheapskate deal like that, thinking that it'll give you a new life somewhere else." Jenner added, "Property prices are pretty insane everywhere right now."

"And they won't get any cheaper," Jim muttered.

"You've got a home. You've got acreage. You can have all the animals you want. Do any number of hobbies. Whatever you wanted to do." Jenner smiled. "We just have to find a way to get you back on your feet again."

"Do you think that prosthetic specialist would talk to me?"

"I know she would," Jenner stated. Then something occurred to him. "How do you feel about dogs?"

"I love dogs," he replied, "but I just don't know that I'll be in any shape to look after them. Most people won't even let me adopt them if I have to go through formal routes. What are you getting at?" Jim asked, a curious note in his tone.

"I'm just thinking about things," he replied.

"Is this about the War Dog?"

"Maybe."

"Well, I know the dogs were there, while the beating was going on. The guy was yelling at them, telling them to get into the truck. I didn't really hear it all," Jim said. "But, when he took off, I thought I still heard one of the dogs kind of sniffling around me. I don't know. It was very weird."

"Interesting," he murmured. "Any chance the dog was all black?"

"It was." He asked, "Why?"

"The War Dog that your parents adopted is black. Whenever the wild dogs came at me—which has happened three times now—the War Dog immediately jumped between them and me," he explained. "So I'm wondering if Sisco didn't do the same thing for you, step in to protect you from those dogs."

"Maybe, I don't know. But I do remember it seemed like the dog was really dark, but that could just be my imagination."

"It's not an issue right now anyway."

"No, but I sure hope you manage to save it."

"I've also got one of the wild dogs at the vet." He quickly brought Jim up-to-date on that.

"Jesus, those dogs really haven't had much of a chance, have they?"

"Nope, sure haven't. How are you with dogs?"

"Great, was raised with them all my life. My parents were trainers."

"Which is how they got the War Dog then," Jenner noted, with that clicking into his brain as to one of the missing pieces.

"Yeah, Dad especially was really good with them," Jim said. "I know they'd have been thrilled if I actually worked with dogs again. But they also couldn't know what it's like in my condition."

"No, they don't," Jenner agreed. "I do, however. And I have faith that you can do anything that you want to do. That house of yours happens to be a great place. Now I'm not telling you to keep this house if it's something that you don't want to deal with. If the memories are too hard or maybe you didn't give a shit about your parents, and this is just another way to put closure to all that, then sell it."

"No, no, no, no," Jim stated immediately. "We actually had a great relationship. I was just the one who was struggling to come home with all the injuries, and I didn't want to be a burden on them."

"I wonder if they would have seen you as a burden though," he asked Jim.

"No, my mom kept telling me to come home, where she could help."

"Of course she did. She's a mom."

At that, Jim, his voice catching, whispered, "I really miss them."

"Good. Everybody deserves to be missed. You don't want to know that you'll die and that nobody'll give a crap," he murmured. "So I'm glad that you will miss them. They deserve that too." At that, he added, "Get better. I'll go. I just took a walk through your place, and it looks like everything is fine. But don't go signing any deals with Silas until you've had a chance to think upon it."

"Yeah, but I am not sure that I've got the money to make the changes needed to the house. I don't have the know-how myself either," he added. "I don't have any support group either."

"Well, I did hear," Jenner said, with a smile, "that a neighbor of yours came by with awesome cookies today."

"Oh my God," Jim exclaimed, "she could make a fortune off her baking."

"And you just had some of her cookies. I ate something wonderful for dinner, and I'm so in love that it's ridiculous."

At that, Jim started to laugh. "It actually sounds like maybe you *are* falling in love."

"Ah, hasn't been enough time for that," he noted, "but she is pretty special."

"You know what? I'm not so sure about that. My parents first met at a party, and they basically were inseparable after that. They said it was love at first sight. I don't even know what that means anymore."

"Do you know any of the people around here?" Jenner asked Jim.

"Sure, I was raised there."

"So you know all about Kellie's mess."

"Teenage pregnancy? Yes, absolutely. The town basically crucified her. It was so ridiculous. She was dating the sheriff's son, and neither the sheriff or his kid would even acknowledge the child. And then after everything that happened with her son," he added, his voice dropping, "I think basically the sentiment was to leave it and her all alone. I know that, for her, it was a really hard time. Her parents came round, but only once they knew about her little boy's illness. Even so, that made life a little easier on Kellie too." Jim added, "The people here are just shitty sometimes."

"They absolutely are, and do you know Laura?"

"Yeah, I do know Laura. That woman's a bitch."

Jenner winced at that. "Really? I guess I didn't know her as well as I thought I did."

"She was one of those who was really good at making you think that you were special, and then, when you weren't looking, you find out that she basically backstabbed you with somebody else."

"Yeah, you could say that." Realizing that Jim deserved to hear the truth, Jenner revealed, "She is my ex-wife."

There was silence on the other end, and Jim asked in wonder, "What?"

"Yeah, we didn't meet here," Jenner explained. "She's the one who sent me a Dear John letter overseas, saying she was divorcing me and marrying my best friend. And I was pretty irate for a very long time, and then I talked to my best friend and realized they never did get married. He was still a shit for having an affair with her, and I wouldn't have anything to do with him since then, but, at the same time, I kind of understood because she was a bit of a force unto herself."

"Yeah, she's also the kind who's not happy unless she has a man in tow," Jim noted. "Sorry you got caught in that trap."

"I think they call it the honey trap, don't they? And now she's married to Silas."

At that, Jim went dead silent. "Seriously, Silas? The one who's offering to buy my property?"

Jenner nodded and realized Jim couldn't see the nod, and so Jenner spoke up. "Yeah, that's the guy."

"Interesting," Jim murmured, "sounds like she's up to her usual tricks."

"Well, she's also pregnant, so maybe this is a good match for her."

"Maybe," Jim said, "but it's sure as hell making me not want to sell to him. Just because of her."

Such disgust filled Jim's voice that Jenner laughed. "Well, don't do it because of me," he stated. "I'm over her."

"Yeah, I hope you are," he murmured. "Besides, Kellie is a hell of a better deal. And a hell of a baker."

Jenner nodded again. "Anyway, I'll let you go. I'll walk through your house again and actually take a closer look at just what would be required to make it wheelchair accessible."

"Yeah, but you also have to count in labor," Jim noted.

Jenner hesitated and then, knowing that there was really no way he would not offer it, he said, "Look. If I stay around, I can give you a hand. I can do this kind of stuff pretty simply."

"What kind of stuff?" he asked cautiously.

"Carpentry work, like for the ramps," he replied, "I spent a lot of summers doing construction work, so it's not like I can do it all for you, but, if you can supply the materials, then maybe we can do something about it. Hell, for that matter, I might be able to get the materials or at least some assistance from the VA to get you back on your feet, back into your own home."

"Do you think there is any help for that kind of stuff?" he asked. "Because that would be huge. Of course you also said *if* you stick around."

"If I stick around, yeah."

"And what makes it an *if*?"

"I'm not sure," he admitted. "First off, I have to rescue Sisco the War Dog. When I do get him back on my side and alive and well, and the sheriff is not gunning for Sisco every second, I'll need a place for him. On top of that? ... Well, I'm getting kind of accustomed to some pretty nice cooking." Hearing Jim's laughter on the other end, Jenner hung up, grinning like a fool.

Shoving his phone in his pocket, he had just the briefest of warnings, and then the dog attacked.

CHAPTER 14

KELLIE WAS OUTSIDE on the rear porch, sitting in the dark, when the front doorbell rang. Frowning, she walked inside to the front door and opened it up to see Silas standing there. She looked at him and asked, "Yes, can I help you?"

He frowned at her. "You have somebody staying here. I would like to speak with him."

"He's not here right now. Did you want to leave a message?"

He snorted. "No, I don't want to leave a message."

She shrugged. "In that case then, you could come back tomorrow. He should be here then."

He hesitated and then said, "Let him know I stopped in and that I would like to talk to him."

"Sure thing," she said, with a smile. He looked around at her place, and she saw the clear disapproval in his expression. "Not to worry," she added, "your wife canceled the reservation."

"I should think so," he replied, with an inward shudder that was so obvious but she knew he'd had a lot of practice at making it look good. He turned and walked away. She wanted to yell behind him some caustic comment about, *It was too good for your relatives anyway*, but knew it would be a wasted effort. And she was better off not making more enemies around this place.

On the other hand, it was also something she needed to do for herself, but, as she stepped out to the front veranda to share her comment with him, he was already in his vehicle and backing out. She shook her head at her hesitation.

As she watched, Silas quickly disappeared, and she sent a quick text message to Jenner. When he didn't answer after a few minutes, she frowned and quickly phoned him. And again he didn't pick up the phone. She hung up and then tried again. And this time, she heard a clatter, almost like he'd tossed his phone, but she heard him yelling and ... fighting with somebody?

She swore, as she turned, raced through her house to the rear door, and headed out to the back of her property. But what was she supposed to do? She listened intently and looked around and then quickly climbed the hill before her. When she got up there, she heard noises, and she headed straight for Jenner, finding him on the ground with Sisco. She frowned. "Wow, okay, I thought something terrible was happening."

"Watch out!" He jumped up and ran toward her.

She turned to see the wild dog, standing in front of her, glaring, saliva dripping off its teeth and fangs, as it howled and then charged her. The scream froze inside her throat, and, before she had a chance to react further, another streak came flying through the darkness and slammed into the wild dog, dropping it to the ground. But the wild dog hopped to its feet really fast, and, instead of turning on her, it turned on its attacker.

Then came a dog fight that broke her heart to see but was absolutely terrifying at the same time. As Jenner reached her side, he gently pulled her out of the way.

"What's going on?" she asked.

"That is Sisco, and, all the while, he's been trying to keep the wild dog in check."

"I don't think it's working."

"No, not only is it not working, chances are good it won't work at all. That wild dog likes the taste of death too much."

"But Sisco saved my life," she said, looking at the black one.

"I know, but right now it'll be damn hard to get Sisco away from this wild dog, without Sisco getting hurt too." In the distance came shouts. "And their presence will complicate matters terribly," Jenner said.

Suddenly there was a shot, a single shot, and then a second one.

Even as she watched the wild dog dropped to the ground, Sisco disappeared into the darkness. "Dammit." She raced after him.

"Stop," Jenner yelled.

The sheriff came racing toward them. "What the hell?" he roared. "How is it we only got one?"

"Well, you got the only one you should be shooting," Kellie yelled back at the sheriff. "The other dog, the War Dog, saved my life."

The sheriff stared at her in shock. "What are you talking about?"

She quickly explained, and he shook his head. "You don't know that it was trying to save you."

"Yes, I do," she said immediately. "He was stopping the other dog from attacking me."

"And the same thing is what happened to me too," Jenner reported to the sheriff.

He stared at him suspiciously. "I don't believe a word of it. I am damn sure that you're just making it up."

"Right, like I make up stories about attacking dogs." Such a dry note was in his voice that the sheriff looked at him and flushed.

"Hell I don't know you at all, and, ever since you've been in town, you've been nothing but trouble."

At that, Jenner's eyebrows shot up. "Oh, now that's a very interesting statement to make. You can always call the navy."

"Hey, I just got off the phone with Silas, and apparently you're making trouble all over the place."

Kellie turned toward Jenner. "Sorry, I forgot to tell you. I didn't get a chance in all of this nightmare, ... but Silas came by the B&B to talk to you tonight."

"Oh that will be fun," Jenner said. "Looking forward to that talk."

And the sheriff snorted. "Silas can handle guys like you, no problem."

"Yeah, I'm sure he thinks he can."

At that, the sheriff flushed and glared at him. "We've got to take care of this dog problem right now, so there'll be a hunt for the other dog."

"Well, you can," Jenner replied, "but believe me. I will be contacting Commander Glen Cross at the war department right now on behalf of that dog," he said, as he retrieved his phone from the grass. "Sisco did exactly what he's trained to do. Sisco saved Kellie, and Sisco saved me earlier. It would be made very public if you shoot that War Dog."

"I didn't say anything about shooting that one," the sheriff seemed to decide on the spot. "I know a third one is around here."

"Well, that one we saw earlier," Jenner admitted. "I don't even think it's alive anymore."

The sheriff stared at him. "What?"

"When I saw it last time, it was limping pretty badly and trailing blood."

"Well then, that makes it even more dangerous."

"I doubt you'll even see it again. It's probably gone off to die in the woods," Jenner noted in disgust. "I sure as hell wouldn't worry about it. This is the one that was dangerous." Jenner pointed at the dead dog nearby. "You should probably get it tested for rabies."

At that, the sheriff frowned, then he shrugged. "I'm not touching it."

"You'll just leave the dog out here?" Kellie asked in shock.

"Sure, the coyotes can take care of it." The sheriff looked around the area. "Coyotes got to eat too." And, with that, he motioned at his deputy and said, "Let's get out of here."

Together they turned and walked away.

"WHAT ARE YOU doing up here?" Jenner asked, roughly pulling Kellie into his arms. "My God, you could have been hurt."

"I know that now," she said, "but, when you dropped your phone, I guess it answered my phone call, and I heard what was going on. It was instinctive. I just came running."

"Well, your instincts need a tune-up then," he noted, with a rough smile. "Because, wow, that's not exactly the kind of reaction I'd have hoped for."

"I wouldn't leave you up here to fight off wild dogs on your own."

"Yeah, what would you do about it?" he asked, as he turned her gently toward home. "Were you going to bake up a storm and feed them?"

"Hey, if it would work," she declared. "I would have brought food in a heartbeat. Why are we going home?"

"Because I want to get the sheriff away from here, and, once Sisco realizes the other dog is out of commission, I'm hoping Sisco will come with us too."

"And will he come home or back to Jim's place?"

"I'm kind of hoping back to Jim's," Jenner replied. "Because, if ever a guy needed a dog for a best friend, it's Jim."

She looked at Jenner and started to laugh. "So you're not matchmaking. You're just ... what's that called?" She pretended to think and added, "Adoption matchmaker for dogs?"

He laughed. "That doesn't sound like a bad thing."

"No, it doesn't," she agreed. "I literally just made it up, but, hey, it sounds good to me."

"Sounds good to you because you're busy being that good person."

"Me?" She shook her head. "I'm not a good person. I've got forgiveness issues. However, *you* are a good person."

"Well, we'll agree to disagree." He looked around and asked, "Are you ready to go home and to grab some shut-eye tonight?"

"Absolutely," she said.

He put an arm around her shoulders and told her, "Watch your steps. It's pretty dark up here."

"I know, and yet, honest to God, I just ran here in the dark, right into the wild dog. I didn't even think about the danger."

"That's good." He turned to look behind him and added, "Don't turn now, but Sisco is following us."

"Oh, that's good," she said, looking at Jenner with joy.

"It is good, but we're still a long way away yet from having this solved."

"I know, but I'll take this as a step in the right direction."

"Not only a step in the right direction, this is progress in a big way."

She nodded. "I can put food out for him."

"I've got lots of dog food at your place. We'll set up regular feedings, and I don't think it would take very long for us to actually get close enough to him."

"What about the sheriff?"

"Well, if we keep Sisco on your property in the backyard, I don't think it will be a problem, but who knows."

"Hopefully that works. I really want to be able to give Sisco a decent life."

"I do too." He leaned over and kissed her on the temple. "Thanks for coming to the rescue, by the way."

She snorted. "Yeah, like I was any help."

"Hey, I think you were a great help. If nothing else it did my heart good to see you there. Of course I also froze, when I saw the alpha dog coming after you," he admitted, "but Sisco here took care of that." He whistled and called the dog forward. And, sure enough, Sisco, after a wary glance at both of them, stepped up to the side of them and walked close enough to actually look like he was walking with them.

"I'm scared to breathe, in case he disappears again," Kellie whispered.

"I don't think so now. I think that closed one pathway

in his life," he murmured. "Whether we really understand it or not, I think he knew the wild dog was dangerous. And so he was trying to make sure that wild dog didn't hurt us. It all started with Jim, saving him from the wild pack."

"I really like that," she said. "I have to admit I'm still nervous around dogs because of what happened. But Sisco here could go a long way to making me feel better." She asked, "Are you looking at keeping him?"

"Depends on Jim," Jenner noted. "So I don't know yet. I mean, we'll see. I do think Jim would be a great partner for Sisco."

"And what about the other one though?"

"It's quite possible that the two of them need each other and Jim."

"But could Jim handle both?"

"Well, in the interim, I think it depends on how long I'm able to stay here and help," he noted, with a chuckle. "I've done some training. Jim's done a lot more than I have. So it's quite possible that, between us, we can make sure the dogs are doing just fine."

She smiled up at him. "You know what? I like the idea of anything that'll keep you around."

"Oh? I was kind of hoping maybe you'd be okay with it," he said. "You know we were kind of making some steps toward that." He pointed at the back porch to the B&B. "Hey, we're already home."

She looked up and frowned. "Too bad. It was just getting interesting." She opened the door and stepped into the kitchen, and, as she heard noises, she turned to see him already dishing out dog food for Sisco.

"You think it'll just be like that?"

"It'll just be like that"—he nodded—"at least for a

while. We'll keep him in the backyard and out of the kitchen, if that's okay with you."

"Totally okay with me. I'd actually prefer it."

And he could sense the nervousness in her voice. "Absolutely. This is your house. Only what you're comfortable with."

She looked over at him and shrugged. "I feel foolish."

"It's not foolish at all," he murmured. "You need to be comfortable in your own space." He grabbed another bowl and added water to it, then took it and the food bowl outside to where Sisco waited patiently. Jenner locked up the gate, so Sisco was within the enclosed backyard—knowing full well Sisco could jump that fence at any time, yet hoping he knew he was safe here—then stepped into the kitchen, closing the door, with the dog outside. "Now, where were we?"

As he turned to face her, she threw her arms around his neck and said, "We were right here." And she kissed him with a passion that went bone deep.

He felt his brain melt and his body heat up, as he wrapped his arms around her and kissed her back.

CHAPTER 15

K ELLIE PULLED BACK and whispered, "Now I don't want to start something that you don't want to finish."

His eyebrows shot up, and he pulled her tighter into his arms and said, "Oh no you don't. You don't get to start something like that and then back away." Then he hesitated, frowned.

She shook her head, reached up, kissed him gently, and whispered, "I'm not backing away from anything. Maybe we'd like to take this upstairs."

"Oh hell yeah." He looked at the stairs behind her and looked around the kitchen and then added, "Too bad you don't have a bedroom on the main floor."

"Ha. I do, but it's not mine. Since you don't know where my room is, you'll have to follow me." And, with that, she laughed and took off running. She was gratified to know, just as fast as she raced forward, he was right behind her. By the time he got to her room, she already had her shirt off and was unbuttoning her shorts. She quickly divested herself of her shorts and then turned to face him in just her bra and panties. She grinned at him. "Now you're way behind."

"Oh, not for long." He pulled his T-shirt over his head, and his hands went to the buckle on his jeans, but she was already there.

"I can't wait." She unbuckled his belt, unbuttoned his

jeans, and lowered the zipper. She pulled the jeans away just enough to wrap her hand around his erection.

And he groaned when he felt her make contact. "Good God, you know it's been a little while for me. I might need some time."

She snorted. "You don't seem to need any time, but we might, you know, do this once or twice tonight before we both get it out of our system."

"You think?" He smirked. "I can't imagine ever getting you out of my system." He half picked her up and half tossed her onto the bed. With a shriek of laughter, she flattened herself out, spreading her arms and legs, and said, "Get down here with me."

But first he kicked off his shoes, shucked his jeans and his boxers and socks, all at the same time, and he ended up half tumbling onto the bed. "Wow, that was graceful," he muttered.

She snickered. "I would take this over a practiced grace any day."

He looked at her in appreciation. "I meant, since my accident ..."

"Good, that puts us on a more even keel."

"It's not a contest," he added.

"No, and I'm glad for that," she murmured. "It's nice to know that you're not always falling into bed with women."

"Because you said ..."

"I haven't done this very much."

"Yeah."

"Just enough to get pregnant," she noted, with an eye roll. "Speaking of which, I'm on the pill," she added immediately.

He nodded. "That's one less thing to worry about tonight." He stretched alongside her on the bed and quickly unsnapped the front closure on her bra. "We'll take care of that real fast too."

She looked up at him, smiling. "If you say so."

"This is a wholesome two-person activity." He leaned over and tugged the bra strap off her shoulder.

She sat up, quickly divested herself of it, and stretched back out again. "It does feel good," she said, as his hand immediately stroked across her ribs. "I hadn't realized just how much I missed being touched."

"It's what we all need," he stated. "Just the touch of human kindness if nothing else. You've been alone for a long time, haven't you?"

She gave him a misty smile. "It shouldn't have felt like that, but in many ways it did."

"Of course it did," he said, as he pulled her closer. "But this is for us," he whispered, and he rolled over and gave her a deep tongue-penetrating kiss.

She shuddered in his arms and realized it wouldn't take very much for her to reach an orgasm, right here and now. She wrapped her arms around his neck and whispered, "Show me."

And, with that, he stroked every inch of her, seeming to kiss every inch of her too but couldn't have because, well, she'd taken over almost immediately. Her own need had risen to his stroking and teasing and touching, before she pulled him closer and tighter into her arms, whispering, "Please now."

He shifted gently. "No, we're not quite ready." Then he straddled her, his arms lifting him above her, as he looked down at her. "My leg'll be in the way."

"Then take it off," she said immediately.

He shook his head. "It's not a pretty sight." She glared at him, trying to pull him closer. He shrugged and gave in to her. "Are you sure?"

"Absolutely." She sat up and watched as he removed the prosthetic and slowly rolled down the protective sock to reveal a still angry red stump. She gave a slight cry, leaned over, and kissed it gently. He grabbed her, pulled her up, and whispered, "The skin's incredibly sensitive."

"Good to know." She lightly ran her fingers over the end of it. "Don't ever be afraid of showing that to me," she said. "My scars might be more inside, but yours at least were received with honest work and a warrior's heart."

He chuckled at that, and then she looked at him and said, "I'm serious. Don't ever try to hide something so simple. It's a part of you. And that won't ever be something that I'll be afraid of."

His gaze darkened, as she stared at him. He pulled her into his arms and whispered, "You're so damn special. You know that?"

"Nope, I don't know that." She gave him an impudent smile. "But you can spend the next while telling me and proving it to me."

"That's a deal," he said, with a bright smile, as he suddenly flipped her to her back, and she gave out a squeal of laughter. And then she caught sight of the look in his eyes, and all her laughter fled. She opened her arms and whispered, "Please."

He lowered his head and immediately took her right back up to a pulse-pounding kiss, as she quivered in his arms, completely shocked how something like this felt so good and took her to an edge so fast. She knew it was all him.

He was the magical element here. How they felt so damn right together. When he settled above her, she opened her thighs, wrapped her legs gently around his hips, and then gently stroked her calves up and down the back of his thighs and whispered, "You're so damn sexy."

He murmured something indistinguishable and plunged deep, centering himself right at the heart of her, and her climax was instantaneous.

He slowly dropped to his elbows and whispered, "Are you okay?"

"I am," she muttered, waiting for her body to calm down. "When I said it had been a while, I meant it."

He nodded. "Good. Hate to be sexist about it, but I'm always happy to know that it's new for you," he said. "*This* feels damn new to me too."

And then he slowly started to move, building up the tempo again, until she cried out in his arms. And only when she had plunged off the cliff for a second time did he follow. As he collapsed in her arms a little bit later, she murmured, "I don't know what that was, but that wasn't like anything I've felt before."

"Good." His breathing was still crazy fast against her chest. "I'm glad to hear that." He half groaned. "And I'll give you a chance to try it all over again, when my breathing calms down. Because, damn it, you almost killed me."

She chuckled. "I don't believe that for a second, but, hey, I'm happy to give you so much pleasure."

He lifted his head, looked at her, his gaze tender but truthful, as he whispered, "It does not feel like anything I've ever had before," he said gently. "Maybe it's the timing. Maybe I had to wait for you. I don't know, but it feels damn right."

At that, she nodded immediately. "I was just thinking that. Not sure how that happened, but it feels like it's meant to be."

"I'll go along with that." He gently rubbed his nose against hers. "And now I think we should try that again. Maybe practice makes perfect."

"It was perfect already," she said immediately. "No practice required."

At the crestfallen look on his face, she burst out laughing. "But that doesn't mean we can't do it all over again, and this time for fun."

He gave her a huge grin. "A woman after my own heart." And he proceeded to show her all over again just how special she was.

As she laid in his arms the second time, she murmured, "I hate to say it, but, damn, I'm hungry."

He raised his head, looked at her, and started to laugh. "And again … I won't argue with that because I am too."

"I have a meat pie downstairs. Maybe we need a piece of that."

"Meat pie?" he repeated, staring at her with hope. "Like, a real meat pie?"

"Yes. You know with pastry and real meat?" She chuckled. "I made it today, when I was getting so worried."

"Well, I sure don't want you to worry unnecessarily, but I'd be tempted to make you worried a little bit if it sets you off to cooking like this."

She chuckled. "Let's go get something." She quickly grabbed a robe off the back of the door and then turned to look at him and frowned. "I should have thought about your leg."

"I'll put it back on again." And sure enough he was rolling on the sock and plunked the prosthetic back on fairly easily. She said, "I feel like you did that haphazardly."

"I take more time normally, but this works for now. Come on. Lead the way. You said, *meat pie.*"

She chuckled and led the way downstairs to the kitchen, and she pulled out the meat pie from the fridge and showed him.

"You were serious." He was almost salivating.

She gave him a big fat smile. "Absolutely. When it comes to food, I'm very serious."

"I've died and gone to heaven," he said, rubbing his stomach.

She laughed, put the pie on a plate and cut two thick slabs and said, "I want it warmed up a bit first."

He nodded, but, hearing something, he stepped to the back door. "This is the only door that leads out to the backyard right?"

"Yes. No. One is in the storeroom there." She pointed to the side. He frowned as he stepped back there.

She followed. "I don't usually use that door."

"Maybe not." He looked down and checked it. "Yet it's unlocked."

"No, I always keep it locked because I never use it. It's always locked."

"No, this one is unlocked," he said, turning to look at her.

She frowned as she walked closer. "I swear to God, I locked it." She opened the door and then closed it again and shrugged. "I don't know when I even used it last. I don't know how long it's been like that."

"That's a disconcerting thought."

"I know." She chewed on her bottom lip.

"Let's not worry about it right now," he suggested. And they stepped back into the kitchen, just as something slammed against the back of his head, and Jenner dropped to the floor without a word. She stared in horror at Jim—or rather whoever it was who had played Jim.

"My God," she said, her hand on her throat. "What are you doing here? Why did you hurt him?" she cried out.

"What do you think?" He looked at the little bit of clothing she wore and nodded. "I knew you'd be hot," he said. "Nothing like those women who get pregnant and get stuck at home ever after. They're always looking for a free ride."

She stared at him, pulling her robe closer together, fear choking her. *No, no, no, no, no.* She looked around, and the rear kitchen door had been left partially opened, when he had let himself inside her home, she presumed. She glanced at the floor, where Jenner was out cold.

"My God, why would you hurt him?" And then the tears came to her eyes, and she glared at her intruder. "Not only why would you hurt him, how dare you hurt him," she said, her voice gaining in volume. "I'm getting really pissed off and fed up with people making assumptions about me when they don't know anything about me at all."

He leered at her. "I know all about you. Rumor has it you got pregnant as a teenager and since then you've been all alone by yourself. Of course that's what this guy is up to. It figures as much. I mean, what the hell though?" He looked down at her. "He's got a prosthetic. He's not even a whole man."

This is the asshole who took down Jim in a surprise attack and left him to die on his own property. She glared at him, feeling the same anger burning inside. She knew exactly what this guy was after, and she would fight him tooth and nail to keep him at bay. But the fact that he'd attacked Jenner took her right over the edge of anger into sheer fury.

"How the hell could you even compare yourself to him?" she asked. "You're the one with those dogs that you hurt, damn near killed them with your behavior. You only staved them off me that one time because somebody was likely to see me get attacked by the dogs in broad daylight," she said bitterly.

"No, I already had you earmarked for later. I'm only in town for this visit. I figured I'd take off right afterward. I'll be long gone, before you even wake up enough to tell the cops about any of this." He laughed. Then he stopped, looked at her and said, "Or maybe I won't let you wake up at all."

She froze, stared at him, and then he lunged. Just like that wild dog of his. She didn't even think about it. She snatched the cast-iron frying pan off the stove—just as something black streaked in the open back door—and she connected with her attacker's head so hard that she heard it ringing in the kitchen, even as Sisco jumped up and grabbed him on the wrist and thereafter came a bone-crunching *snap*.

At the same time, she saw Jenner climbing to his feet, pushing off the wall, as he tried to get to the intruder.

Except the asshole had dropped to the floor and never made a sound. She stood still, the frying pan in her hand, as she stared at Jenner. "Oh my God, I think I killed him." And then she dropped the frying pan and raced into his arms. And he wrapped them tightly around her, and he whispered, "Good. Saves me the job."

She looked up at him and muttered, "Oh my God, oh my God."

"It's okay. Dead or alive, it was self-defense. Even better, we have him now, thanks to you. And he won't walk away from any of this." She buried her face against his chest and whispered, "Dear God, that was awful."

"And yet look at you. You're hell on wheels in the kitchen with a frying pan, even when not cooking. Look at that."

She burst out laughing. "I absolutely am apparently." She looked down at the asshole and smiled. "I hate to say it, but you know that, this time, we'll have to call the sheriff."

"Absolutely we will," he said, with a note of satisfaction. "But this time, it's all good."

"If you say so, but what if he sees Sisco out back?"

"The War Dog saved you yet again, which is exactly what Sisco was trained to do," Jenner added. "So it's even better than all good. Honest to God, I think this is the best ending possible."

"No. I disagree," she said. "Being in your arms like this? This is the best ending possible."

"Sweetheart, this isn't an ending. This is a beginning."

EPILOGUE

BADGER LOOKED OVER at Kat, as they sat in their living room, and asked, "How did you get to be so smart?"

"I didn't get to be smart at all," she said. "I just knew something was there about his ex-wife, but I had no idea that he just needed to make peace with her. I figured he needed to deal with something."

"Well, not only did he make peace with her—in the sense that they have spoken and have agreed to ignore each other—but her much-older husband is also not so happy to have her younger ex-husband in town. So Silas is chomping at the bit over that." Badger laughed. "Not to mention the squatter seemed to do this elsewhere. Jenner did the sheriff's job and checked in nearby counties, so that guy is sitting in jail, and the sheriff's not happy to be shown up by Jenner either. But better than that, Jim is home, and Jenner will stay in town to help him fix up the place for wheelchair access."

"I think that's a great idea." Kat looked over at Badger. "Is there any spare money to help out with some supplies?" Badger rolled his eyes at her. She grinned and added, "Well, I'll help out with the prosthetic. I just figured that maybe they needed some building supplies to handle the modifications."

"Absolutely they do," Badger agreed. "I'll talk to the guys about it."

She nodded. "You do that."

Such a note of satisfaction filled her voice that he grinned at her. "You, my dear, are one very manipulative prosthetic genius."

"Only when it counts." She walked over and sat down on his lap, wrapped her arms around him, and said, "Besides, it's a happy story all around. How can we not like that?"

"It's perfect. Jim'll keep both dogs at his revamped childhood home, and even Kellie is getting comfortable being around them. I don't see Jenner being dogless for long."

"No, and I think it's a great idea that Jenner sets up a way to help veterans. I mean, it'll take some time to coordinate, but he'll be somebody else for us to send people to."

"Ah." Badger laughed. "You've got a soft heart, my dear."

"I do, but the good thing is, it belongs to you." She wrapped her arms tighter around him and kissed him. Then she twisted in his arms and asked, "What's this?" She pointed to the end table beside them.

"The next file."

"Wow. Have you got somebody for it?"

"Nope, not yet. Jager thought he might know somebody. One of his neighbors. I guess their son came home, looking a little worse for wear."

"Right. It's hard to imagine how many out there aren't even on our radar."

"Well, this guy came back from a mission over in Iraq, got blown up—a story we all know—and maybe he needs to talk to you. I'm not so sure yet, but apparently a dog over there died in the same accident and he's really heartsick over it. They were moving the forward operating base, when they got blown up. So he's looking to find something else in his life to find meaning."

"Oh, I like this already. Where will we send him?"

"*We?*" he asked, raising his eyebrows.

"Absolutely. This is a *we* job."

He smiled and agreed. "It is, indeed."

"And where's the dog?"

"In Oregon."

She frowned at that.

"Why, what's wrong with Oregon?" he asked her.

"Oregon's fine, but I hope it's an okay scenario for our War Dog and our next man."

"This *is* a different scenario. We haven't had one of these before."

"And what does that mean?"

"Apparently a woman picked up the dog, contacted the ASPCA, found it was tagged, came up as one of the War Dogs, and they want somebody to go check on it."

"She wants to keep it? Because, if that's the case, it would be a good thing. Right?"

"She does want to keep the dog but is concerned about its training. She hasn't had much."

"What about this guy you are sending? Has he any experience with K9s?"

"Well, he was a trainer, so, in a way, it's a match made in heaven."

She looked up at him, and a glint came into her eyes.

He nodded. "I know you wouldn't miss that reference. Apparently she's also ex-military, and she's got her own prosthetic. Although she's struggling with it and was hoping this dog would be more of a therapy animal."

Kat's frown flashed again. "I don't know that the War

Dogs have that kind of temperament."

"I don't think she's looking to get it registered, just more of a case of she's alone and could use it for mental health purposes, like an emotional support dog."

"In that case, you're right. It sounds like a match made in heaven."

"I hope so, but I've got to get a hold of this guy first."

Just then came a knock on the open door, and Jager walked in and pointed. "This is actually him. *Rhys.*"

The man leaned against the doorframe, his arms crossed over his chest.

"The one I was telling you about."

"Right." Badger nodded. He looked over at Kat and then at the closed file. He asked his wife, "What do you think?"

She studied Rhys and decided immediately. "Let's do it."

This concludes Book 16 of The K9 Files: Jenner.

Read about Rhys: The K9 Files, Book 17

THE K9 FILES: RHYS (BOOK #17)

Welcome to the all new K9 Files series reconnecting readers with the unforgettable men from SEALs of Steel in a new series of action packed, page turning romantic suspense that fans have come to expect from USA TODAY Bestselling author Dale Mayer. Pssst… you'll meet other favorite characters from SEALs of Honor and Heroes for Hire too!

Rhys hadn't expected a trip to Cottage Grove, Oregon to start with a house being shot up with bullets. If it had stopped there it would have been manageable. A drive by shooting that the cops should be able to chase down. But nothing was easy in his world. And this case went to hell right from the beginning…

Taylor, an army vet herself was struggling to regain a normal life after she was injured by friendly fire in Iraq. Taking on a war dog appealed as it gave her a connection that they could both relate too, but she had to pass some kind of interview before she could keep Tallahassee. An interview with someone with a prosthetic just like hers. Only he was far more capable than she was.

Still that was the least of her worries as things go from bad to worse and she realizes these attacks were very personal… and very close to home…

Find Book 17 here!

To find out more visit Dale Mayer's website.

https://geni.us/DMRhysUniversal

Author's Note

Thank you for reading Jenner: The K9 Files, Book 16! If you enjoyed the book, please take a moment and leave a short review.

Dear reader,

I love to hear from readers, and you can contact me at my website: www.dalemayer.com or at my Facebook author page. To be informed of new releases and special offers, sign up for my newsletter or follow me on BookBub. And if you are interested in joining Dale Mayer's Reader Group, here is the Facebook sign up page.
http://geni.us/DaleMayerFBGroup

Cheers,
Dale Mayer

Get THREE Free Books Now!

Have you met the SEALS of Honor?

SEALs of Honor Books 1, 2, and 3. Follow the stories of brave, badass warriors who serve their country with honor and love their women to the limits of life and death.

Read Mason, Hawk, and Dane right now for FREE.

Go here and tell me where to send them!
https://dalemayer.com/masonfree/

About the Author

Dale Mayer is a *USA Today* best-selling author, best known for her SEALs military romances, her Psychic Visions series, and her Lovely Lethal Garden cozy series. Her contemporary romances are raw and full of passion and emotion (Broken But ... Mending, Hathaway House series). Her thrillers will keep you guessing (Kate Morgan, By Death series), and her romantic comedies will keep you giggling (*It's a Dog's Life*, a stand-alone novella; and the Broken Protocols series, starring Charming Marvin, the cat).

Dale honors the stories that come to her—and some of them are crazy, break all the rules and cross multiple genres!

To go with her fiction, she also writes nonfiction in many different fields, with books available on résumé writing, companion gardening, and the US mortgage system. All her books are available in print and ebook format.

Connect with Dale Mayer Online

Dale's Website – www.dalemayer.com
Twitter – @DaleMayer
Facebook Page – geni.us/DaleMayerFBFanPage
Facebook Group – geni.us/DaleMayerFBGroup
BookBub – geni.us/DaleMayerBookbub
Instagram – geni.us/DaleMayerInstagram
Goodreads – geni.us/DaleMayerGoodreads
Newsletter – geni.us/DaleNews

Also by Dale Mayer

Published Adult Books:

Shadow Recon
Magnus, Book 1

Bullard's Battle
Ryland's Reach, Book 1
Cain's Cross, Book 2
Eton's Escape, Book 3
Garret's Gambit, Book 4
Kano's Keep, Book 5
Fallon's Flaw, Book 6
Quinn's Quest, Book 7
Bullard's Beauty, Book 8
Bullard's Best, Book 9
Bullard's Battle, Books 1–2
Bullard's Battle, Books 3–4
Bullard's Battle, Books 5–6
Bullard's Battle, Books 7–8

Terkel's Team
Damon's Deal, Book 1
Wade's War, Book 2
Gage's Goal, Book 3
Calum's Contact, Book 4
Rick's Road, Book 5

Kate Morgan

Simon Says… Hide, Book 1
Simon Says… Jump, Book 2
Simon Says… Ride, Book 3
Simon Says… Scream, Book 4
Simon Says… Run, Book 5

Hathaway House

Aaron, Book 1
Brock, Book 2
Cole, Book 3
Denton, Book 4
Elliot, Book 5
Finn, Book 6
Gregory, Book 7
Heath, Book 8
Iain, Book 9
Jaden, Book 10
Keith, Book 11
Lance, Book 12
Melissa, Book 13
Nash, Book 14
Owen, Book 15
Percy, Book 16
Quinton, Book 17
Hathaway House, Books 1–3
Hathaway House, Books 4–6
Hathaway House, Books 7–9

The K9 Files

Ethan, Book 1
Pierce, Book 2

Zane, Book 3
Blaze, Book 4
Lucas, Book 5
Parker, Book 6
Carter, Book 7
Weston, Book 8
Greyson, Book 9
Rowan, Book 10
Caleb, Book 11
Kurt, Book 12
Tucker, Book 13
Harley, Book 14
Kyron, Book 15
Jenner, Book 16
Rhys, Book 17
The K9 Files, Books 1–2
The K9 Files, Books 3–4
The K9 Files, Books 5–6
The K9 Files, Books 7–8
The K9 Files, Books 9–10
The K9 Files, Books 11–12

Lovely Lethal Gardens
Arsenic in the Azaleas, Book 1
Bones in the Begonias, Book 2
Corpse in the Carnations, Book 3
Daggers in the Dahlias, Book 4
Evidence in the Echinacea, Book 5
Footprints in the Ferns, Book 6
Gun in the Gardenias, Book 7
Handcuffs in the Heather, Book 8
Ice Pick in the Ivy, Book 9

Jewels in the Juniper, Book 10
Killer in the Kiwis, Book 11
Lifeless in the Lilies, Book 12
Murder in the Marigolds, Book 13
Nabbed in the Nasturtiums, Book 14
Offed in the Orchids, Book 15
Poison in the Pansies, Book 16
Quarry in the Quince, Book 17
Revenge in the Roses, Book 18
Lovely Lethal Gardens, Books 1–2
Lovely Lethal Gardens, Books 3–4
Lovely Lethal Gardens, Books 5–6
Lovely Lethal Gardens, Books 7–8
Lovely Lethal Gardens, Books 9–10

Psychic Vision Series

Tuesday's Child
Hide 'n Go Seek
Maddy's Floor
Garden of Sorrow
Knock Knock...
Rare Find
Eyes to the Soul
Now You See Her
Shattered
Into the Abyss
Seeds of Malice
Eye of the Falcon
Itsy-Bitsy Spider
Unmasked
Deep Beneath
From the Ashes

Stroke of Death
Ice Maiden
Snap, Crackle...
What If...
Talking Bones
String of Tears
Psychic Visions Books 1–3
Psychic Visions Books 4–6
Psychic Visions Books 7–9

By Death Series
Touched by Death
Haunted by Death
Chilled by Death
By Death Books 1–3

Broken Protocols – Romantic Comedy Series
Cat's Meow
Cat's Pajamas
Cat's Cradle
Cat's Claus
Broken Protocols 1-4

Broken and... Mending
Skin
Scars
Scales (of Justice)
Broken but... Mending 1-3

Glory
Genesis
Tori
Celeste

Glory Trilogy

Biker Blues
Morgan: Biker Blues, Volume 1
Cash: Biker Blues, Volume 2

SEALs of Honor
Mason: SEALs of Honor, Book 1
Hawk: SEALs of Honor, Book 2
Dane: SEALs of Honor, Book 3
Swede: SEALs of Honor, Book 4
Shadow: SEALs of Honor, Book 5
Cooper: SEALs of Honor, Book 6
Markus: SEALs of Honor, Book 7
Evan: SEALs of Honor, Book 8
Mason's Wish: SEALs of Honor, Book 9
Chase: SEALs of Honor, Book 10
Brett: SEALs of Honor, Book 11
Devlin: SEALs of Honor, Book 12
Easton: SEALs of Honor, Book 13
Ryder: SEALs of Honor, Book 14
Macklin: SEALs of Honor, Book 15
Corey: SEALs of Honor, Book 16
Warrick: SEALs of Honor, Book 17
Tanner: SEALs of Honor, Book 18
Jackson: SEALs of Honor, Book 19
Kanen: SEALs of Honor, Book 20
Nelson: SEALs of Honor, Book 21
Taylor: SEALs of Honor, Book 22
Colton: SEALs of Honor, Book 23
Troy: SEALs of Honor, Book 24
Axel: SEALs of Honor, Book 25

Heroes for Hire

SEALs of Steel

The Mavericks

Griffin, Book 2
Jax, Book 3
Beau, Book 4
Asher, Book 5
Ryker, Book 6
Miles, Book 7
Nico, Book 8
Keane, Book 9
Lennox, Book 10
Gavin, Book 11
Shane, Book 12
Diesel, Book 13
Jerricho, Book 14
Killian, Book 15
Hatch, Book 16
Corbin, Book 17
Aiden, Book 18
The Mavericks, Books 1–2
The Mavericks, Books 3–4
The Mavericks, Books 5–6
The Mavericks, Books 7–8
The Mavericks, Books 9–10
The Mavericks, Books 11–12

Collections
Dare to Be You...
Dare to Love...
Dare to be Strong...
RomanceX3

Standalone Novellas
It's a Dog's Life

Riana's Revenge
Second Chances

Published Young Adult Books:

Family Blood Ties Series
Vampire in Denial
Vampire in Distress
Vampire in Design
Vampire in Deceit
Vampire in Defiance
Vampire in Conflict
Vampire in Chaos
Vampire in Crisis
Vampire in Control
Vampire in Charge
Family Blood Ties Set 1–3
Family Blood Ties Set 1–5
Family Blood Ties Set 4–6
Family Blood Ties Set 7–9
Sian's Solution, A Family Blood Ties Series Prequel
     Novelette

Design series
Dangerous Designs
Deadly Designs
Darkest Designs
Design Series Trilogy

Standalone
In Cassie's Corner
Gem Stone (a Gemma Stone Mystery)

Published Non-Fiction Books:

Career Essentials

Career Essentials: The Résumé
Career Essentials: The Cover Letter
Career Essentials: The Interview
Career Essentials: 3 in 1

Made in United States
North Haven, CT
01 December 2022

27647170R00135